'No, Jack!' ... ... calmly.

Jack merely c... ... looked down i... ... Rosie,' he said. His voice was cloud-soft and dangerous—as were his eyes. 'Despite everything I still want you. So I shall begin wooing you all over again. Starting tonight.'

'Jack, you don't really want *me*. You can't!'

'Oh, but I do.'

Dear Reader

As summer gives way to autumn, this is a good time to reflect on how you feel about your loved ones. Being in love can be the most wonderful feeling on earth, yet why is it that so many people are frightened of expressing that love? That's certainly the case between our hero and heroine, yet, as in life, once expressed, it can lead to the greatest happiness. I think there's a lot to be learned in our books. Have fun learning ...!

The Editor

Jenny Cartwright was born and raised in Wales. After three years at university in Kent and a year spent in America, she returned to Wales where she has lived and worked ever since. Happily married with three young children—a girl and two boys—she began to indulge her lifelong desire to write when her lively twins were very small. The peaceful solitude she enjoys whilst creating her romances contrasts happily with the often hectic bustle of her family life.

Recent titles by the same author:

RELUCTANT SURRENDER
STORM OF PASSION

BITTER POSSESSION

BY
JENNY CARTWRIGHT

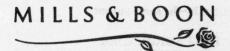

MILLS & BOON

MILLS & BOON LIMITED
ETON HOUSE, 18-24 PARADISE ROAD
RICHMOND, SURREY TW9 1SR

*First published in Great Britain 1993
by Mills & Boon Limited*

© Jenny Cartwright 1993

*Australian copyright 1993
Philippine copyright 1993
This edition 1993*

ISBN 0 263 78267 0

*Set in Times Roman 10 on 11¼ pt.
01-9310-57551 C*

Made and printed in Great Britain

CHAPTER ONE

IT HADN'T happened for two years. Before that she'd
often found her eyes snared by a silhouette, an outline,
a glimpse of a dark head—inches taller than the crowd.
Then her mouth would parch, her heart would drum
with fear and she would turn and walk briskly in the
other direction. Just in case it really was him. Just in
case he saw her and caught up with her and spoke. So
when it happened again—and in Dorchester, of all
places, on a September's afternoon—she was quite taken
aback. Fortunately, after all this time, she hadn't responded with the old panic. In fact, she had quite easily
convinced herself that it couldn't really have been him
in that car at all. Not after four years. And certainly not
in Dorchester.

He had been behind the wheel of a car when she had
seen him for the first time. But it had not been the sombre
black machine of a businessman then. The car was a
two-seater convertible, very sporty, cream, with a navy
hood. It had swooshed along close to the ground on its
fat tyres, sending gravel skidding out in all directions as
it slewed to a halt on the driveway.

Rosie had been on her knees, weeding the border in
front of the house, when the car—or more properly, its
driver—intruded on her consciousness that hot July
afternoon. One brief glance at the face watching her from
the driver's seat had been enough to bring a warm flush
creeping up her cheeks. He was the most attractive man
she had ever seen in her life. He had pulled into the

driveway of her home and he was looking at her. Any minute now he was going to speak. She could tell. She ran her tongue over her lips as she rubbed the worst of the earth from her hands on to the back pockets of her jeans. And then wished she hadn't.

'Hi,' he said lightly, opening the door of the car and swinging out first one unbelievably long leg and then the other. He was dressed in a pair of olive gabardine trousers and a soft denim shirt with the sleeves rolled back. With his thick, dark, straight hair brushed back from his high forehead and his tanned skin, he looked the epitome of casual elegance.

'Hello...' returned Rosie nervously, trying not to glance down at the weathered pink T-shirt streaked with grass-stains and the ancient jeans. Her own appearance might well be casual, but elegant it most certainly was not.

He was coming towards her. She scrambled to her feet, anxious not to appear at too great a disadvantage. Though why she should care what he thought was beyond her comprehension. It wasn't as if... Well, the trouble was that although she was nearly twenty—just a couple more months to go now—she had only weeks earlier left her convent school. She was still wrapped around by a whole host of schoolgirl dreams about tall, dark, handsome strangers. It was quite absurd—she was perfectly aware of that—especially as he must be at least thirty and had probably come to see her father about something... But she still couldn't help wishing that she were lounging in a wicker chair on the lawn right now, wearing a flowery sundress, reading poetry and sipping iced lemon tea.

'I'm lost...' he said, sauntering towards her. 'I'm trying to get to Dorchester, but I've been driving around these lanes for what seems like hours.'

Rosie found herself wishing that there were a blizzard raging. She could have ushered him into the house then and offered him hot soup and a bed for the night.

'Ah...Dorchester...' she said vaguely as if she only dimly remembered ever having heard of the place. And then she pulled herself together and added briskly, 'It's really easy, actually. You turn left out of the driveway and then you go along a bit and then there's a turning on the right. I think it's the first, if you don't count the road which goes to the Haywards' farm because that's a dead end—but it might be the second. And then after a bit—well, quite a long way really—there's a sort of humpbacked bridge just after the road you need. You'll know if you've gone the wrong way because you'll go past a church.'

He raised his hands defensively, palms outwards in front of his face, as if staving off an onslaught. 'Hey...hey...hold on a minute.'

She pulled a rueful face. 'I'm sorry,' she said. 'Can't you follow what I'm saying? I'm not very good at giving directions, I'm afraid. The trouble is that I've lived here all my life and I know instinctively where things are without having to think about it, let alone put it all into words—if you know what I mean.'

He smiled a dry, amused sort of smile which set his blue eyes dancing.

'Oh, I know what to do!' she exclaimed with a sudden rush of inspiration. 'I'll come with you and show you the way. It'll be much easier.'

He was probably cringing inwardly at the offer although he was politely keeping that nice smile on his face. But so what? A man like him would hardly be interested in a girl like her. *She* knew that. She wasn't completely self-deluded. But at least she would have the excitement of riding alongside a man like him in a wonderful little car like that on a day like this. It would be great fun, and he would be none the wiser. There would be no harm done.

'How will you get back?' he asked.

'I'll get a bus. I need to go into town anyway. There are some things I need to buy.'

'Haven't you been advised not to accept lifts from strange men?' he cautioned, with a wry smile.

She grinned. 'I've been awfully badly brought up, as it happens. You can ask anyone around here—they'll all confirm it. Anyway, I've invited myself. It's not the same thing at all.'

He gave a low growl of laughter. 'Oughtn't you tell someone where you're going?'

Rosie shrugged. 'There's only my father. He'll be absolutely furious if I disturb him.' He was working like crazy, trying to get some last-minute work completed. 'Anyway,' she continued blithely, 'he'll be off to Australia in a day or so. I'll be on my own then. He won't care.' Her father trusted her, knowing that she was a level-headed girl. At any rate, she had loads of old schoolfriends she could stay with if she got fed up.

He was frowning. Oh, dear... He must be trying to find a way to wriggle out of it. If only she'd been sitting in that non-existent wicker chair, sipping the iced lemon tea she didn't even know how to make, and with her hair swept into a chignon—whatever that might be...

Despite being at least five feet six inches tall Rosie somehow managed to look no more than eleven years old most of the time. Her long silky nut-brown hair was drawn back to her nape in a thick plait, secured with a length of green garden twine. The line of her high, rounded forehead was invariably interrupted by disobedient tendrils of hair. One corkscrewing wisp fell directly over her short nose, which itself curved slightly upwards from the bridge to the tip where it broadened a little, giving her the air of a young animal. A fawn or a kitten, maybe. Open, curious and very, very young.

She blew the offending tendril away, protruding her generous lower lip to do so. 'I come and go as I please,' she explained, wondering how to let him know that she was older than she looked without actually spelling it out. 'I'll be leaving home in October, as it happens. To go to university. I should have gone last year, actually, but I did an extra year at school.'

There! You didn't need to be a mathematical genius to work that one out. She smiled broadly in what she hoped was an assured and confident manner. The smile, besides revealing a set of large, but even and perfectly white teeth, went straight to the huge, dark brown eyes which dominated the curves and hollows of her sun-browned angular face. Rosie, dark-eyed, willow-necked, slender, had still, at nineteen—to her chagrin—the fresh, untouched beauty of childhood about her.

Still he hesitated. 'Isn't there anyone else?'

She looked at him in surprise. Didn't he believe her? 'No. My mother's gone.'

He continued to frown. Oh, help! Had she made it sound as if her mother were dead? That was awful . . .

'Er—she's not around any more,' she added brightly. 'She's gone away. Abroad. She's remarried. She's very happy. Very happy indeed. Extraordinarily happy.' Good. That was better. She'd made her mother sound extremely alive. She didn't want to give the impression that she was some kind of tragic little orphan Annie on top of everything else.

He continued to study her almost suspiciously with those astute blue eyes, rimmed around with a dense line of short black lashes. Then his regard lightened a little and he said, 'Well, if you're going to come along and show me the way we'd better introduce ourselves. I'm Jack. Jack Hellec.'

'Rosie Wells,' breathed Rosie, biting on her lip to stop herself from smiling too obviously. Jack ... Oh, it really suited him. Jack Hellec. Yes. She flashed him a brief grin then hurried towards the car before he had a chance to change his mind.

She was just about to open the passenger door when his hand came out to detain her. So he'd changed his mind after all? Ah, well ... Back to the weeding ...

He let his hand rest gently for a moment on her bare forearm. Then he said drily, 'Excuse me, Rosie ...' And he took his hand from her arm and used it to brush briskly at the seat of her jeans. 'That's better,' he concluded with a very broad smile.

Rosie almost jumped out of her skin as the palm of his hand slapped at her jeans-clad bottom. And then she remembered wiping all that earth off her hands on to the back of her jeans and realised what he had been doing. She knew her face was bright red—she could feel the heat radiating from it. In fact, she suspected that her entire body must be blushing, because she could feel heat radiating from every inch of her skin, too.

They were halfway to Dorchester before she dared turn her head to look at him again. The breeze was whipping his hair back from his face. There were fine grey streaks here and there among its dark perfection, she noticed. Not just the odd grey hair, but proper streaks. They made him seem even more worldly and experienced somehow. His cheekbones were high, his brows straight, his mouth well shaped beneath a deeply cleft upper lip which, even closely shaved, bloomed faintly blue. And those deep-set blue eyes which had scrutinised her so keenly in that moment before he had brushed the earth from the seat of her jeans ... How on earth did one set about impressing someone like him? She couldn't even pluck up the nerve to start talking to him again. She turned her eyes back to the summery landscape which, for once, didn't seem quite as impressive as usual. It must have paled into insignificance beside him, she found herself thinking; and quashed a giggle.

Just before they arrived in the town centre she remembered that she had no money on her. She surreptitiously slipped her long fingers into first one and then the other of her jeans pockets and felt around anxiously for a forgotten coin. Not a bean. And, of course, he chose just that moment to look at her as they waited in a traffic queue.

'What's the matter, Rosie?'

'Nothing.'

'You look worried.'

'Do I? I think I may have a basset hound among my ancestors. People often say I'm looking worried when I'm not.'

'You haven't any money with you, have you?'

'Er—well...'

'Go on. Admit it.'

'The thing is, it doesn't actually matter. I have a friend, Cathy, from school. Her father has a greengrocer's shop. Even if she isn't in, Mr Banes will be in the shop and he'll lend me some.'

They were driving through the quaint streets of the old market town now. Jack pointed to a pretty tearoom across the street. 'I'll see you in there,' he said firmly, glancing at the clock on the dashboard of the car, 'at five-thirty. If you arrive before me, order yourself something. I'll pay when I arrive. *And* I'll drive you back home.'

'Really, I'm fine. Honestly. I know hundreds of people in Dorchester, and——'

'Five-thirty. That's an order.'

Rosie nodded her mortified agreement. She had only wanted a brief ride on a sunny day in an open-topped sports car with a tall, dark, handsome stranger. It was meant to be no more than an uncomplicated treat for the more juvenile side of her psyche. This was dreadful. She hadn't meant to inconvenience him and force him to drive her all the way back home, too. Oh, she *was* a fool . . .

He turned up a few minutes after her, transformed into something even more enigmatic and austere by a suit and tie. She hadn't ordered anything, not wanting to impose. He made a disapproving noise when he realised what she had done, and then proceeded to order tea and scones for them both.

'Tell me about yourself,' he said, breaking a piece off a scone and buttering it.

'What do you want to know?'

He shrugged, leaning back in his chair and looking intently into her eyes. 'I don't know. Why did you spend an extra year in school, for instance?'

Rosie rubbed at the side of her nose with the middle finger of one hand. Oh, dear. It wasn't an easy question to answer. 'I . . . I repeated the fifth year and did resits.'

'But you're not dumb. You've got a university place, after all . . .'

'Er—yes. Well, I had a few distractions to cope with that year. Family problems.'

'Ah. Your ecstatically happy mother, I presume . . .'

Rosie winced. She hated talking about all that. It had been bad enough living through it. She'd learned to accept it, but it hadn't been easy. Her mother had fallen in love with another man. Her dear mother whom she'd loved and trusted. Even that wouldn't have been *so* bad. These things happened, after all. She'd known her mother wasn't going to leave. After all, she'd had an affair with this chap once before, apparently, and had broken it off. She hadn't gone the first time round, and she wasn't going to leave this time, either. Rosie knew because she'd overheard her talking to her elder daughter,

Rosie's sister Emma. Mum had been crying, saying that she couldn't break up the family. That she'd get over it in time. But Emma—Emma, *unbelievably*—had actually been encouraging her. 'You must go with him, Mum,' she'd said. 'Take me with you,' she'd pleaded. 'We can make a new life. It will work out. I promise. Please. Please, Mum. Please. You must. You love him. You do.' She had gone on and on until Rosie had almost been sick.

'Yes. Sort of,' responded Rosie non-committally. 'Anyway,' she added more brightly, 'I didn't want to ruin my education just because of a temporary hiccup. So I did the extra year. It was great, really, because I got to know all the girls in the year below me and made a new set of friends. It's silly, isn't it, the way that people don't make friends with people just because they're a year younger? Or, at least, that was the way it tended to be in my school... Cathy Banes, the one with the shop—well, I'd hardly spoken to her before then and now we're really good pals.' Rosie abruptly stopped herself talking and sipped at her tea. Trust her to have gone rabbiting on about school like a child. Still, it was better than rabbiting on about her mother and her sister. She could hardly bear to look at Jack, though. He must think she had a mental age of about nine.

He didn't say much after that, not in the tearoom nor in his car. He certainly didn't ask her to tell him all about herself again. She'd really blown that one. There was so much she could have said that would have sounded much more mature and sensible. Her interest in history, and her plans for the garden, for instance. So it was a complete surprise when he pulled into the driveway again and actually got out of the car with her.

'I can see myself in,' she said apologetically, convinced that he must be thinking her a complete imbecile.

'I'll come in and wait,' he responded. 'You can get changed and I'll take you back to my hotel for a meal.'

Rosie's eyes opened wide. 'Good grief!' she exclaimed. 'That's very kind. But you don't need to. I've been enough trouble as it is.'

'It will be my pleasure,' he said softly, and smiled an encouraging smile.

Rosie felt almost weak with excitement as she led the way into the capacious Victorian house and through to the sitting-room. Her father was still in the old stables, chipping away at his blocks of stone, and the housekeeper had taken the opportunity of her father's impending departure to take a holiday of her own. As she rushed upstairs to get changed she realised that she should have offered him a drink instead of just leaving him there all alone. She hesitated for a moment. Should she go back down? No. She'd hurry and get dressed really quickly. If she dragged things out too much he might change his mind and go.

She arrived back in the sitting-room, quite breathless, but transformed from an urchin by a crisp white broderie anglaise dress, her hair falling silkily over her shoulders to the middle of her back.

'I know I should have offered before,' she said, 'but would you like a drink?'

He shook his head. 'No, thanks.' He glanced at his watch. 'Come on,' he said, 'let's get going. You look lovely.'

The compliment almost had her melting with pleasure. Honestly, how was she going to cope when she finally got to college if her head was so easily turned by a throwaway compliment from a man who wasn't really interested in her at all? He'd told her earlier that he was in Dorchester for a couple of weeks on business. Even *her* company must seem an improvement on a long evening alone in his hotel in this sleepy, little town. Once

she was surrounded by students she would have to take
care not to make a fool of herself over the first young
male to set his cap at her. Especially if he turned out to
have blue eyes. Because it was beginning to dawn on
Rosie that she must have a peculiar susceptibility to blue
eyes in a man, judging by the way she was reacting to
Jack's.

And it got worse as the evening progressed. When he
took her arm to lead her to the table she felt almost faint
with the thrill of it. His touch was light and warm. It
brought her out in goose-bumps. And then, when his
hand brushed against her waist as he seated her, she felt
something new, something powerful, thumping through
her like an electrical charge. Her skin tingled and deep
inside a new, very special warmth was fountaining upwards. I have been awakened, she thought excitedly as
he came around to sit opposite her. Until a moment ago
I was still a child. Now I am a woman.

The feeling stayed with her throughout the meal. It
was a wonderful feeling. A waiting feeling. A feeling
biding its time, promising, at last, to become something
more. She watched the way his mouth moved when he
talked; the way he filled the space opposite her. She
watched his large hands fingering the silverware, and
breaking his bread. The feeling surged slightly as she
saw his lips move, his chest expand slightly with every
breath, his fingers gently tearing at the crust. The feeling
was anticipating a time when there would be no damask-
clothed table between them; when she would touch rather
than watch the space occupied by his body. And extraordinarily, as the meal progressed from course to course,
she became increasingly convinced that he, too, foresaw
that time, and was waiting with her.

He asked her again about herself. Exhilaration made
her voluble. She laughed and bit at her lip and told him
all sorts of things. This time, though, she was careful

to steer her revelations away from that ruptured, wounded time in her life. And he told her about his French-Canadian grandfather and the property business over there and him—Jack—being British, really, but his father going abroad and then Jack going too, to learn the business from the bottom, and then coming back to expand the British and European side. Rosie didn't take much of it in. She was too preoccupied with watching him, and waiting.

When he delivered her back home he touched her elbow several times as he handed her in and out of the car. But he didn't kiss her. Oddly enough, she was pleased. He was so much older than she. So much more experienced. She was glad that he was waiting, too.

'I've got to spend a couple of days in London on business,' he said as he left. 'But I'll be in touch.'

And again, oddly, she wasn't disappointed. Somehow she just knew it wasn't an excuse. As soon as he stopped being busy he would come and see her again. There was something about the charged atmosphere of the evening which left her with no doubts.

Her father was waiting for her when she got back home.

'Been anywhere nice?' he asked, rubbing benignly at his beard.

'Mmm....' she replied, then burst out, 'Oh, Dad! I think I'm in love.'

He pulled a face, an amused, pleased sort of face, and said, 'Well done.'

'Is that all you've got to say?'

He shrugged. 'What am I supposed to say?'

'I don't know. You're the father. You must know what to say when your daughter comes home and says she's in love for the first time.'

'Oh.' He looked surprised. He furrowed his brow and scratched a bit more at his beard. Then illumination beamed out of his eyes. 'Don't forget to go on the Pill,' he said humorously.

'Dad!' She positively wailed the word. 'You're not supposed to say that at all. Especially since *you* were the one who chose to bring me up in the heart of the country. You can't raise a daughter in such a sheltered way and then say things like that. I'll end up neurotic. Really!'

He sighed ruefully. 'So come on, Rosie. Tell me. What should I say?'

'You're supposed to ask about his prospects and everything, I think.'

'Why? Has he asked you to marry him?'

'No. Of course not. I've only been out with him once.'

'Well, then . . .' He put out an arm to hug her around the waist and added, 'It's a good job I've got you to tell me how to bring you up. We'd both be in a right pickle without each other, wouldn't we?'

She returned his hug affectionately. She'd miss him while he was away, even though she was eager for a taste of independence. He had been so marvellous when her mother and Emma had left. So resolute and strong for her, despite his own pain. He spoke of them both with such tenderness that Rosie guessed he couldn't know how heartlessly Emma had rejected him. She avoided mentioning the subject, afraid she might inadvertently reveal the truth about her sister. It could only hurt her father to find out what Emma had done, and would do no good at all.

'Are you going to be all right while I'm away?' her father asked gravely.

'Of course. You know I will. Why do you ask?'

'Oh, I don't know. I figured that falling in love might have changed your mind.'

'Good grief. You must be joking! It will give me something to do while you're away. And will also mean that I don't have to introduce you to him.'

'Why? Wouldn't I approve?'

'Of course you would. I have just discovered that I have impeccable taste in men. But apparently in well-regulated households one is expected to bring one's True Love home for Sunday tea. You always get very irritable, Dad, on Sundays. Especially around teatime. You hate the weekend radio programmes. You say they interrupt your routine and you can't concentrate on your work. You stomp around and grind your teeth. Remember?'

CHAPTER TWO

WHEN Jack did return, a few days later, he was wearing a suit again. A light grey suit this time. Rosie had been up in her room, trying to figure out the complexities of the chignon.

'Hi,' she said when she opened the door to him, then added admiringly, 'You look great.'

He frowned. 'That was supposed to have been my line. Except that you don't.'

Her long-fingered brown hand flew to her hair and extracted a few of the more peculiarly placed hairpins. She smiled weakly.

His own hands reached out behind her head and extracted the rest. And then he arranged her hair over her shoulders and bent his face to hers and kissed her.

Rosie's eyes closed against the blue of the sky, blocking out the flutter of green leaves, the blur of his skin. And as her eyes closed so her lips parted. It was her first real kiss. She had always been afraid that when the time came she wouldn't know what to do. But his warm, dry lips brushing against her mouth; his moist, powerful tongue, probing against hers with a careful restraint, provided all the tutoring she needed. The unfamiliar pressure of his shaven chin against her own sent desire leaping hot and dark into her veins. That feeling, held in abeyance, began at last to unfold its mysteries to her.

When they broke apart his mouth travelled delicately over her face, leaving a trail of small kisses in its wake before he straightened up. He smoothed her hair with his broad hands. She found herself shivering with pleasure as she leant her cheek against his chest. He was so tall. He seemed to tower over her. It meant that her ear was pressed to his heart, hearing the steady thump, sensing the reassuring swell of his breathing.

'That was wonderful,' she sighed shakily.

'Good. It was meant to be. Now go and get changed into something disreputable. I'm taking you for a special evening out.'

She looked up at him, mildly shocked. 'Disreputable?' she queried archly. 'I don't exactly go in for those kinds of clothes...'

The blue eyes which met hers glittered humorously. 'Rosie!' he muttered reprovingly. 'What on earth did you think I meant? A strapless sheath-dress in scarlet satin? What in heaven's name is going on in that head of yours?'

'I——' She pressed her lips together, then sighed. 'So what *do* you mean by disreputable?'

Two lines hooped down his cheeks when he smiled his reply. 'Oh, just jeans with a muddy patch at the back. A baggy pink T-shirt decorated with grass-stains. Scuffed trainers. You know the sort of thing. Anything but that ghastly floral creation you've got on.'

Rosie looked mournfuly down at her sundress. She'd bought it in Dorchester just the previous day. Admittedly it wasn't the sort of thing she usually chose. This time, though, she remembered to provide him with a drink before she dashed upstairs to change. Hopefully she'd got that part right, at least. But when she returned downstairs in a pair of blue matelot trousers with a matching stripy sweatshirt and navy deck shoes—all of which she'd bought long before she met him, with only her own taste in mind—it was to discover that he'd left the drink untouched.

He looked at her appreciatively. 'Now that's a lot better,' he said.

'Don't you want it?' she asked anxiously, nodding towards the glass.

He grimaced. 'I have to admit it doesn't quite suit my palate. What is it?'

'Iced lemon tea,' she replied, trying not to laugh out loud at herself. She chewed on her lower lip, but it did no good. The laughter bubbled up regardless.

He surveyed her quizzically. 'What's the joke?'

'Um...' Rosie bowed her head and scratched her forehead, trying to quell her mirth sufficiently to speak. She pointed at a calf-bound volume of poetry lying open on the sofa. 'I—er—well, I may as well admit it,' she said quaveringly at last, 'I bought the dress and pinned up my hair and made the iced tea in order to impress you with my cool and sophisticated inner self.'

'Where does the book come in?'

'I was planning to be found reading it when you arrived. Except I should have been sitting under the beech trees on the lawn in a wicker chair. I haven't got round to buying the chair yet, though. I'm still saving.'

A smile crackled across the mirror of his eyes. 'Were you so sure I'd come?'

She nodded.

Then he laughed too, and said, 'In that case you really must have a cool and sophisticated inner self, regardless of the outward appearance.'

Oh, well, she thought happily. Perhaps he *did* like her the way she was, after all.

They drove down to Weymouth. He took off the jacket of his suit and slung it over one shoulder. Then he slung his other arm around her shoulder. She could smell his aftershave, faintly citrus against the male tang of his skin. They walked along the quayside, looking at the bob and bustle of the boats.

'I shall buy a little yacht,' he said, 'and take you sailing.'

She glanced down at her clothes. 'I've heard of designer accessories,' she sighed wryly, 'but isn't buying a boat just to go with my outfit carrying extravagance a mite too far?'

Then they visited the fairground, where he encouraged her to sample the rides. Finally, as the late July dusk began to swarm in the air, he walked her into the extraordinary world of Radipole Lake, where high rushes grew like a forest around them, and waterbirds called blindly from the dense reedbeds which stretched out all around. It was a poor destination to choose at the end of a warm summer's day. No sooner had he begun to nibble at her ear than the gnats began to follow suit.

It didn't matter. It made them both laugh, and, anyway, Rosie knew that he would wait. The next day he came back again. And the next and the next. And each time he came he kissed her. Once or twice or three times. And each time her pulses raced, and desire pinched and nipped at her senses in ways she wouldn't have imagined possible. And all the time she knew she was falling more and more deeply in love with this extraordinary man, who was far too old at thirty—and certainly far too sophisticated—to be interested in a girl like her. It was heady, exhilarating, ecstatic. She didn't dare hope that he might feel the same. Oh, she entertained him with her flow of chatter and her self-deprecating jokes. And she was sure that he felt something—a good deal more than something, if she were honest—when he kissed her. But not love. Yet for the moment it didn't matter. It was enough to be held by him and to be taken sailing by him and brought flowers by him. It was the stuff dreams were made of, and she was, after all, too young to do much more than dream.

It was Saturday. Which meant that he didn't have to wear a suit, and which also meant that he came after lunch instead of late in the afternoon. The weather was holding, and Jack complained that the traffic on his way over had been dreadful. Everyone, it seemed, was heading for the coast.

'That's OK,' said Rosie cheerfully. 'We don't need to go anywhere. There's a lake at the bottom of our garden. You can't see it from the house because of the trees. Come on. I'll show you.'

They took cushions from the house and half filled the punt with them.

'I wish you'd liked that flowery dress,' she sighed as she settled herself on the cushions. 'That and a straw hat would have done wonders for my image. And a crumbly chocolate bar, of course.'

'Those shorts do *quite* enough for your image as far as I'm concerned,' he growled, using the pole to push them clear of the bank.

She coloured, but only very slightly. She was getting much better at taking compliments in her stride. Unrequited love had its uses, after all.

Later, when they were both lying on the cushions, drifting free in the middle of the lake, she looked up at his eyes. The afternoon sun was behind him, throwing his face into dark shadow against the ethereal blue vault of the sky. His weight pressed against her, the hard muscles of his thigh crushed between her own. Her T-shirt was rucked up. The last kiss had spoken a passion, an urgency, which had loosed restraints. She wore no bra, so that the hard, excited peaks of her breasts were exposed, dusky and swollen against the milk-white mounds. She was aroused almost to the point of desperation—almost to that threshold where her mind would relinquish all dominion, releasing her into a new world where sensation would be her master. With her last remnants of control she whispered, 'No...' against the nearness of his shadowed face.

He groaned, achingly, desperately, the hollows of his eyes deepening as his face contorted with a kind of pain. Then the thrilling tension of his lean, hard body subsided, and he slumped, anguished, on top of her. Her mouth pressed against the skin of his chest where his shirt had tugged open. Dark, curling hairs sprang into life against her mouth. The tip of her tongue tasted salt and sweat and raw, animal desire on his skin. She turned her head to one side, assailed so strongly by her own need that she was afraid she might weaken. Deep inside her an expectant pulse thudded blindly, still aspiring, still beating out the rhythm of what might have been.

Jack rolled to one side, letting the sun replace the warmth of his flesh on her skin.

'It's OK... It's OK...' he moaned caressingly. 'Don't worry, Rosie. Only when you want me, my love. Only then.' His voice was still thick with unslaked desire.

She turned her huge dark eyes to his face then, and saw the price of his tenderness written in the pained thinning of those lips which had, just moments before, hung ripe and heavy over the swelling buds of her breasts. Tears spilled on to her cheeks.

'I want you now, Jack,' she admitted ingenuously. 'I want you so much I can't bear to deny it. It's just that——'

His finger came up to silence her mouth. 'I love you...' he said softly.

'Oh, and I love you, too,' she returned, whispering earnestly, her generous mouth breaking into an uncertain smile. He couldn't mean it, of course. He was probably just saying it to be kind, but who cared? It sounded so wonderful, murmured so gently, so breathily, so close to her ear that the words waved fine tendrils of hair against her skin.

'I think we had better get married, don't you?' His voice was even softer, even more tender this time. 'Then you won't have to say "no" ever again.'

The words brought so sharp a pleasure leaping up behind her breastbone that she cried out aloud. She hadn't once allowed herself to believe that it could be possible. Not ever. She blinked back tears of happiness while he cradled her fiercely in his arms.

He had to go away on business for the next few days. Rosie wafted around the house and gardens in a stupor of delight. Occasionally she would ask herself why he was interested in a girl like her. But she didn't take the question very seriously any more. He was interested— very interested—and that was enough. He liked her the way she was. He wanted to marry her. What doubts could there be?

When he returned he kissed her so deeply, so urgently, that she whispered, 'Yes!' against his cheek. But he only drew back and smiled into her eyes. He loved her. It was incredible, but she believed it none the less. It had to be true. Then he produced a small white leather box from his pocket and said, 'I've brought you a ring from London... It was one of the reasons I went.'

'But you could have bought a wedding-ring in Dorchester. They're all pretty much of a muchness, after all.'

He had just smiled with a dry amusement, and waited for her to open the box. It was a sapphire and diamond engagement ring. Discreet and very beautifully wrought, the stones were still large and glitteringly impressive.

Rosie looked at it, quite stunned. 'Oh, Jack,' she breathed, her lower lip quivering, 'it's beautiful.'

'It's symbolic of all the beautiful days and nights that are promised between us...' he murmured, slipping the ring on to her finger.

She looked away from him, suddenly made shy by the depth of her emotion. She fingered the little white box. 'What shall I do with this?' she muttered, flustered, not knowing what to say next. 'It's too nice to throw away... Oh, I know...'

And that was when she had run to fetch her mother's jewel-case. Her mother had left it for her when she'd gone, with a brief, apologetic note pinned to the lid. As always, when Rosie fingered the worn red leather box, it brought the recollections swimming back. She had never contacted her mother—how could she when she still felt so much hurt on Emma's account? It would only lead to rows and she would far rather have happy memories.

And yet something she'd read in a magazine recently had given her hope. Emma had had her appendix out some months before they'd gone. She'd been quite poorly, and in this article it said that occasionally peritonitis after appendicitis could lead to infertility. Perhaps the doctors had had to tell Emma something of the sort? And that had made Emma so grief-stricken and so jealous of Rosie that she hadn't been able to stop herself... ?

Well, it was possible, after all, and if that was how it had been then at least Rosie could sympathise a bit. And if she could sympathise a bit then perhaps she might come to sympathise a lot, and in the end perhaps they could all be friends again... ? She glanced down at the sapphire and diamonds, bright against her golden skin. What wouldn't she give to be able to show her mother this ring...

She hugged Jack when she arrived back, and grinned and said, 'Look, I'm a woman of substance. I've even got a proper jewel-case to keep my ring box in. It will be the most precious thing in there.'

She put the case on the kitchen table and opened it. 'Shall we telephone my parents and tell them?' she asked eagerly.

Jack was frowning. There was a pause. 'No...' he said slowly. 'No. Let's surprise everyone. Let's just keep the wedding special to the two of us... I know I'm selfish, but I want to keep you all to myself for as long as possible...'

He took a few of the old rings from the box. Diamonds, sapphires, rubies, emeralds, all set in the heavy, soft gold of bygone ages. Then he took out the Edwardian pearl collar—bands and bands of tiny pearls, designed to encircle a long, slender neck, sweeping out to cover the throat, dipping almost to the breasts, sitting like a mantle on the shoulders. There were intricate Victorian pendants, elegant Georgian necklaces and bracelets, cameos and earrings, brooches and dress clips.

'These must be worth a fair bit,' Jack said gravely.

Rosie shrugged. 'I suppose so. It's a sentimental collection, really. Each generation drops something with memories attached into the box. Some of them are real jewels. Others are simply mementoes, like this strange bracelet. It was woven from my great-great-grandmother's hair—or was it my great-great-grandfather's beard? It's a bit late to find out, now, isn't it? Anyhow, I think most of the stones in the good pieces are real. Though perhaps they're paste? They could be. Not that I have the first idea what paste might be.'

Jack was still studying the pieces, absorbed.

'Paste...' she continued speculatively. 'Ugh! You can't imagine anyone mistaking *paste* for real jewels, can you? It's such an awful, opaque sort of word. Toothpaste; wallpaper paste; flour and water paste; just add water and mix to a thick paste... That sort of word.'

He held an emerald earring up to the light. 'These aren't paste, anyway. That's for sure. Where do you keep them?'

Rosie looked longingly at him. She wished she'd never got them out now. They were boring. She didn't want him to be looking at some old stones. She wanted him to be gazing into her eyes. 'In the wardrobe in my mother's old room,' she sighed. 'They're supposed to be mine since she left, but they're only sort of borrowed. I'm supposed to hand them on to my daughter when I have one.'

She blushed prettily at that point. She and Jack hadn't got round to discussing babies, and she was sufficiently young and innocent still to find the whole subject rather embarrassing. And yet she hoped that he might pick up on her remark. Say something that would let her know that one day—even if it weren't for ages—he'd like a daughter too. For a moment she thought he *was* going to say something like that. There was a moment's hesitation, and then he seemed to change his mind and instead muttered disapprovingly, 'In the wardrobe? But Rosie, this house doesn't have a security system! Isn't there even a safe?'

Rosie shook her head.

Jack rolled his eyes in pained disbelief. 'Not even a simple burglar alarm...' he groaned. 'Oh, Rosie!' he muttered, beginning to put the pieces back in the box. 'I'm going to put this little lot in the bank for a while, until we sort something out.'

Rosie shrugged agreeably. 'OK. But why?'

'For my peace of mind.'

'But I don't care about them.'

'No. But I care about you. I don't want you being burgled. It's not a pleasant experience.'

'I suppose not...' she murmured doubtfully. She'd never given the matter any thought, but she was sure Jack must be right. 'Well, if you think it's for the best...'

'I do.'

He took her to London the evening before the wedding, and booked them separate rooms in a large West End hotel. He filled her room with roses, and had delivered the most exquisite of wedding gowns, complete with a seamstress to guarantee the fit. He even ordered a bouquet of white rosebuds entwined with ivy, and a candy-striped box containing white silk and lace underwear, trimmed with blue ribbons, and finally some kid slippers beaded with pearls. When she was finally dressed, standing enraptured in front of the huge mirror, admiring herself while at the same time nervously wriggling her shoulders, left bare by the unexpectedly low-cut neckline of the dress, Jack appeared behind her with the pearl collar from her jewel-case in his hands.

'Something borrowed,' he said as he placed the pearls around her throat, letting the weight of the necklace drape across her shoulders like a cloak. He fastened it deftly then stood back. She looked at herself again. The meshwork of pearls looked almost like lace against her golden skin, meeting the neckline to perfection at its scalloped edges. Now she was not just suitably modest, but beautiful, virginal, and above all gloriously, radiantly bridal.

He stood beside her, immaculate in morning dress. 'I shall not kiss you,' he murmured roughly, 'until you are truly my bride.'

Rosie made her vows in a little chapel with her heart brimful of happiness. And then Jack lifted her veil and kissed her. He took her straight back to the hotel then, and laid her on the bed, and brought her to the brink of delight and then beyond. For the first time she escaped with him into that timeless space which was whiter than light, unblemished sensation, made brilliant by starpoints of ecstasy. She was his wife in every sense of the word. She hadn't asked for any of it. She had been expecting a homely register office, a dress from her own suitcase, a simple gold band. It would have sufficed. And yet, freely, unasked, he had given her the world.

They were lying in bed in the middle of the afternoon, reading newspapers. Jack had tried to persuade her to go on a shopping spree, but it was wet and windy outside and she preferred to stay indoors and make love yet again.

The telephone rang. He leant across her and picked up the receiver. He had quite frequently taken business calls in the three days since their wedding, so she wasn't surprised. He was awfully good at fobbing the people off. Nobody ever persuaded Jack to do anything he didn't want to do.

This time, however, was different.

'On our honeymoon,' pouted Rosie, pulling him back into the warmth of the bed.

But he was wryly insistent. And so she stopped pouting, finding herself smiling with pleasure at the sight of him dressing on the far side of the room. It was, after all, rather nice to have a husband who had important business matters to attend to.

'I'll be an hour or so,' he had said. 'What will you do with yourself while I'm away?'

Rosie had sunk back on to the mound of pillows, tucking one hand under her cheek. 'First I shall have a lovely long bath. And then I shall go out for a walk and remind myself that the outside world still exists.'

'But I thought you didn't want to go out in this weather?'

'That was when I had something better to do with my time, and someone to do it with . . .' She smiled.

But the very instant that he had gone she realised that she had forgotten to tell him that she loved him. It was the first time that her husband had left her side since their marriage and she hadn't even given him a peck on the cheek! With a mischievous grin she threw on trousers and a sweater and kicked her feet into a pair of canvas shoes before chasing out into the hotel corridor and down to the foyer.

Once there she looked around swiftly. Was she too late? Had he gone? It was a huge space, bustling with people. Pillars and archways and potted palms broke up the vast area. It took her a moment to realise that he not only hadn't gone, but was in fact very close by, on the other side of a veritable hedge of greenery. She recognised his voice.

She was about to run round and take him by surprise when her attention was caught by what he was saying.

'And I love you too. Really. You *have* to believe me...' He was speaking with a strange intensity—almost a fervour—underlining his words.

Puzzled, she edged closer to the bank of foliage and peered through. He was with a woman. He had his arms around a woman. A woman she knew. True, she hadn't seen her for three years. But it would take a lot longer than three years for Rosie to forget her own sister.

Emma cuddled into the crook of Jack's arm. 'I'm sorry, Jack,' she sighed. 'I know I shouldn't have come running here like this. But I felt so alone—so isolated, just waiting for you to come back and make everything all right. It's been awful.'

'It won't be much longer, Emma, I promise,' he had murmured tenderly. 'It will all be all right soon. It really will.'

Emma sighed, then smiled up at him, looking into his eyes. 'I know. I shouldn't be such a fool. I do trust you,

Jack, you know that. Tell me how *you* feel,' she said gently.

He gave a low, soft laugh. 'I feel wonderful,' he said, hugging her closer to him. 'I feel as if I'm walking on air. Love is very special...'

And Emma smiled a self-satisfied smile and stood on tiptoes then, and snuggled against him and kissed him tantalisingly on the cheek. Then she sighed again and said cajolingly, 'But how much longer, Jack? I don't think I can bear much more. If you only knew how I felt...'

'But I do,' he reassured her insistently. 'If I didn't feel the same way, do you think I would be going on with all this deception? But you must learn patience, Emma. It will take time. It'll work, you'll see. And then we can be together again.'

'Oh,' Emma sighed. 'It's all so exciting... Is she pregnant yet, do you think?'

'Emma!' He laughed indulgently. 'Patience, patience...'

Emma laughed too. 'I know I'm being absurd, but I can't wait to be an... well, I shall be a good deal more than an *aunt* when the time comes, won't I? It will be *your* child, Jack, not just Rosie's. Oh, anyone can have a common-or-garden niece or nephew, can't they? But this baby will be practically the same as one of my own, won't it? Do you blame me for being excited at the prospect? Oh, I can't wait for the three of us to be together...'

Jack sighed. 'Oh, Emma... I'm so happy. Just wait a little longer, huh? I'll make sure everything comes right for you. I promise. There'll be no more separations. No more time apart. No more heartbreak... All the wrongs of the past will be put right, and you'll be truly happy at last. I'll look after you, Emma. Always. You know that.'

Rosie had quite unconsciously begun to walk backwards during this last speech of Jack's. She didn't want to hear any more. She felt faint. Any minute now she might keel over. But no. She wouldn't do that. There would be a fuss, a crowd, and Jack would know that she had heard, and she didn't want... Oh, God. She didn't know what she wanted. She just wanted to turn back the clock. It was too hard to breathe in here. There wasn't enough air in this damned place. She needed to get out. Fast.

The London streets were awash with rain. She must have looked dreadful, her face blotched with tears, her clothes drenched. At least on the streets of central London no one took any notice. The storm finally passed, and with it the intensity of Rosie's grief. Instead she found herself becoming quite cold, both inside and out. Horribly cold. Rising up inside her was a wild, intemperate gall, an acrid bitterness which dragged at the corners of her mouth and soured her tongue. The very thought of Jack and Emma together sickened her. How could they have been so despicable? He had married her to provide himself with the child Emma couldn't give him. And later, after the birth? What were they planning to do then? Would he have taken the baby and gone to Emma, or would he have stayed with her, living out a mockery of a marriage, seeing Emma whenever he could, waiting, perhaps, for an excuse to divorce her...?

Just thinking of the possibilities disgusted her. And to imagine she had loved this man! Oh, what a fool she had been... But then she hadn't really loved him... couldn't have... She had simply been too naïve... too easily swept off her feet by the first good-looking man to dazzle her... She had known from the start that he couldn't really be interested in her... She had mistaken a sexual attraction for the real thing, too inexperienced to know the difference. Suddenly she was glad that they had made love so desperately and urgently these past three days. Emma might have captured his soul, but Rosie was returning him to her with his body marked by *their* passion...

She ran resolutely back to the hotel, her feet slapping on the wet pavement. Good. He wasn't in the room. Hurriedly she changed into dry clothes and began packing. She was busily piling garments from the bed into the case when he returned. From where? Another hotel room? The arms of another woman? Oh, God, it all made her feel ill.

'Rosie!' Jack exclaimed, his eyes encompassing the scene. 'What the hell is going on?'

'Try guessing,' she muttered nastily.

'Hey, but Rosie, darling... What's——?'

'Sorry, Jack, but all of a sudden I've gone right off the idea of being married to you. I'm sure you understand how these little things happen. A man of the world like you.'

There was a silence. Rosie kept her eyes firmly on the suitcase. Anything rather than look into Jack's eyes. She had no stomach for it.

'You saw me with Emma?' There was a quiet certainty in his voice. 'You know about our...our relationship?'

'Yes.'

'Look, Rosie, you're upset now, but later we'll talk... It's natural that you should be feeling like this...' And he put his arms around her and nuzzled his face against her neck.

It was as much as she could do not to cry out. White-faced, she kept her lips pressed tight together while she wrenched herself away from him. 'Natural?' Her voice was rich with choking anger. 'You're damned right it's natural. Give me one good reason why I should want to be your wife any more. Or the mother of your children,

come to that. Thank goodness I went on the Pill as soon
as you asked me to marry you. At least I've been spared
that particular horror. Now get out of my way. And my
life.'

'You want a reason for staying? Ah, Rosie, but you
love me . . .'

Even now he thought he could win her round. God,
he must think she was stupid! 'Love you? Oh, no, Jack.
You couldn't be more wrong about that.' And suddenly
she turned to look at him, her eyes cold with hatred. 'I
never loved you. Not for one minute. I was fooled
by . . . by sexual curiosity. That's all. You forget how young
I am—how sheltered I've always been. I wanted to know
what it was like to . . . to sleep with a man. And when
you've had a convent education there's a tendency to
think of marriage as the only way of finding out. In the
circumstances, Jack, your offer seemed temporarily irresistible. Well, I've found out all I need to know about
sex, thank you.' And with that she wrenched the rings
from her fingers and threw them disdainfully at his feet.
'It wasn't worth the expense of those trinkets, I can
assure you,' she jeered.

His expression had darkened, and a sullen colour was
creeping up his neck. No wonder he looked so furious—
his nasty little scheme had just gone up in smoke. His
hand came out to grab at her wrist, but she stepped abruptly away.

'Don't you dare lay a finger on me, Jack, or I'll scream
the place down. Or throw up. It depends which instinct
surfaces first.'

'Rosie . . .' His voice was hoarse with anger. 'Listen . . .
Just because you saw me with Emma——'

But again Rosie couldn't bear to listen to him. That
voice of his which had turned her bones to water—she
didn't want to hear it ever again. 'Emma? I'm glad I
saw you with Emma,' she spat. 'Glad. But don't you

understand that she's the least of it all? Seeing you with her simply opened my eyes to the real reason why I was stupid enough to let you put those rings on my finger. I was inexperienced and curious. If you'd pressed me to sleep with you before the wedding I probably would have done, and saved us both a lot of inconvenience. Now, unfortunately, we are both burdened with an obsolete marriage.' She slammed the case shut. 'Now get out of my way. I have the rest of my life to get on with.'

CHAPTER THREE

ROSIE dropped down a gear, letting her little white Fiesta trail slowly along the last length of country road before turning into the driveway of Littlebourne Hall. She was really quite nervous if the truth be known. She knew she was good at her job. She knew she had all the experience she needed to tackle so large a commission. And it was four years now. Four years since her sister and that man had ripped her confidence to shreds. Mostly she felt that time had served her well. She had healed pretty much without scars. But at moments like these—driving to meet a new client and see a new house—she was reminded that there were still threadbare patches on her soul.

She sighed. Perhaps redecorating the Hall would prove beneficial? She'd known the old house since her childhood. She loved the place. She couldn't help but enjoy working here. Aubrey had given her a good build-up with the new owners—it was bound to work out well, and maybe, at the end of it, she would find her confidence as perfectly restored as the house itself. Once she got talking with the client or his wife she'd soon relax, anyway.

None the less, when she drew up outside the rambling, ivy-clad house, she couldn't resist sneaking a glance in the driver's mirror to reassure herself. She was wearing a loosely cut suit in a heavy, slubby sort of wild silk. It was the violet-grey of a sultry, thundery sky, speckled with the ochre and umber of rain-drenched earth, and teamed with a fine silk camisole in rich, pure violet. Round her head was knotted another piece of fine silk, dyed in stripes of the same colours, a tail of silk cascading down her back with her hair. The headband was a marvellous touch. It made her look stylish, slightly arty, and much more mature. Good. It was just exactly how she needed to look if she was to make the right sort of impression.

The housekeeper answered the door and helped her take her samples and portfolio through into the faded grandeur of the drawing-room. Rosie chose not to sit. Her anxiety was beginning to get to her. She didn't want to appear at a disadvantage when the client arrived. Her eyes fixed themselves on the door while she waited out the long minutes.

And then he appeared. The door simply opened and he came through it. That car... That sleek black car, weaving through the streets of Dorchester on a September afternoon...? With a chilling sense of shock she realised that she *hadn't* been wrong, after all. And now he was here in front of her, coming through the door, and this time there was nowhere to turn; nowhere to run. And oh, it *hurt* seeing him walk into the room. It hurt just as it had in the hotel room that day. Four years—and the agony of seeing him was every bit as sharp as it had been then. There was a tightening behind her breastbone—a pain as if someone were opening her heart.

He was tall. Six three or four. She'd forgotten how tall he was. And so grandly male despite the expensive grey suit which smoothed the rangy muscularity of his frame into expertly tailored elegance. His thick, straight dark hair had been cropped shorter, masking more readily the occasional swaths of grey which streaked maverick-fashion through it. The high cheekbones, the straight brows, the well-shaped mouth, configured just as they had been then, combining together to create the very face which Rosie had loved almost at first sight. And the eyes. Oh, his eyes. They hurt her more than anything If time had taught Rosie one thing, it was that she *had* loved him, after all, before she found out.

He was coming forward, his hand outstretched. And then he stopped abruptly, his hand clenching into a fist and lowering slowly to his side, his eyes widening and then darkening.

'Rosie? My God, Rosie? Is it really you?'

Her mouth was frozen. Her tongue stuck to the roof of her mouth. Then slowly, coldly, she offered her own hand to be shaken.

'Rosamund Wells,' she said formally in a voice so stiff that it almost cracked under the pressure of being used. 'I can't say I'm pleased to meet you. It would be dishonest. But will "How do you do?" suffice instead?'

'Dammit, Rosie, I know who you are!' His own voice grated sharply, like steel on granite.

She lowered her rejected hand, pressing the open palm hard against the side of her thigh. Thank goodness he hadn't taken it. Seeing him was bad enough. To have been touched by him would have been way, way too much. Then she turned mechanically towards her portfolio, and stooped to pick it up. 'I'll be going,' she muttered sourly. 'I'm sorry to have wasted your time.'

'Rosie!' His voice was charged: harsh.

She glanced up at him. She could feel the small muscles of her face contracting, drawing tight around her mouth like purse-strings. She was frightened to speak. If she opened her mouth she had no idea what sound would come out. A wail...? A roar...? All she knew was that words were beyond her. She hefted the large portfolio under her arm.

'What the hell are you doing?'

'I...' She took a steadying breath and swallowed hard. 'I'm going. I told you that. I wouldn't have come if I'd known. Aubrey didn't mention any name.'

'Aubrey? Aubrey Greenslade?'

She nodded, taking a few steps towards the door. It had been a mistake to move. Like a watchful animal he pounced, slamming his hand hard upon her arm and taking the portfolio from her.

'*You're* the talented young designer from Chrysalis Interiors?'

She gave a single, haughty nod, then tried to take a few more steps towards the door. But his hand bit fiercely into her arm.

'You're not going yet,' he said decisively. 'I thought we might find an opportunity to renew our... acquaintance when I bought this house. The moment has merely arrived a little sooner than I anticipated. We have a lot of talking to do, Rosie. Four years' worth.'

Her eyes blazed as she looked up at him. 'What on earth can we possibly have to say to one another? As far as I recall, our last conversation was quite conclusive. I came here to work. As that's clearly not going to be possible I wish to leave. Now let go of my arm. You're hurting me.'

'Not possible? Oh, no, Rosie. I'm not letting you walk out again.'

'You can't stop me.'

'I have a contract with Greenslade Weatherall which includes you. It's a start.' He freed her arm.

She gathered it to her and rubbed at the tingling imprint of his fingers on her flesh. It hadn't hurt. Not really. But the searing remembrance of his touch on her arm was worse than any pain. She flashed him a scornful look.

'A contract? If you think any contract in the world would make me stay a moment longer in your presence than I have to, you must be crazy. Our marriage was a contract, after all, and that didn't amount to much, did it? Or have you forgotten all about that?'

He stood back, leaning his hips against the back of a chair, folding his arms nonchalantly across his chest. He was surveying her with a decided coolness now. 'Oh, no,' he said softly. 'I haven't forgotten. And you clearly haven't either. We're still legally married, after all.'

'Only because the five years aren't up yet. The moment they are I shall divorce you.'

'You could have divorced me long ago, Rosie. You don't have to wait for five years.'

'You do if you want a nice, anonymous postal divorce, as well you know.'

He scrutinised her even more coldly. Then he nodded at the portfolio, propped against the chair. 'Shall we get down to business?'

She stepped towards it and once again attempted to pick it up. He didn't touch her this time, merely intruded his large frame between her and the folder. She froze.

'Excuse me,' she muttered with as much icy politeness as she could muster.

'I'll sue the architects if you breach the terms of the contract.'

She eyed him disdainfully. 'Do what you like. Aubrey's an old family friend. He won't mind when I explain the circumstances to him.'

'Aaahhh . . .' A small smile worked at the corners of his mouth. 'So that's why he was so eager to persuade me to let you do the work. So much for your exceptional talents, eh?'

Rosie gasped, biting hard on her lower lip. A huge gush of pride welled up inside. 'Absolutely not.' Her voice quivered a little with an embryonic anger. 'Greenslade Weatherall are the top architects in their field. They wouldn't dream of recommending anyone who didn't meet their standards.'

Those straight brows lifted minutely. He shrugged. 'I don't doubt you're good. But I also don't doubt that Aubrey's judgement is a little biased where charming young female friends of the family are concerned. Men of his age often get a little woolly-minded when beautiful women are involved.'

'What exactly are you implying?'

That shrug again. 'Don't get so worked up. I'm not suggesting that you two have been having an affair. Merely that he might be predisposed to think more highly of your abilities than he would have when he was twenty years younger.'

The anger had matured. Making a wide circle to avoid coming any closer to him than she had to, she marched decisively around him and pushed her portfolio flat on the floor. Then she got down on her knees beside it and flung it open.

'That,' she said vehemently, stabbing at the photograph which lay on top. She flicked it over. 'And that, and that and that. Go on. Look. Decide for yourself.' She leant back on her heels, folding her arms.

He came and crouched down beside her. The muscles of his thighs stretched taut the fabric of his trousers. The leg nearest to her brushed lightly against the edge of her jacket. She stared at that evidence of his physical presence for a brief second then got hastily to her feet and went swiftly to fetch her box of samples. With her back to him and his concentration locked on to the photos and drawings he wouldn't be able to see the faint tremor in her fingers. She felt sick with self-disgust. There it was still, leaping dark and dangerous in her blood. Carnal desire. He still provoked that need in her. Oh, how could she be so stupid?

She returned, opened the box and began to deal the brittle tiles like playing cards on to the worn Turkish carpet in front of him.

'Hey...' he said warningly. 'Careful, Rosie. You'll break them.'

'Over your head, preferably,' she muttered.

'Surely they're worth more than that?' he countered wryly, picking one up and studying it.

But she shook her head. 'Cheap at twice the price. The more precious the item smashed, the greater the satisfaction. That's what makes Laurel and Hardy so funny...'

He placed his broad hands over his knees, threw back his head and laughed. Fine lines fanned out from the corners of his eyes. New lines. His eyes glittered behind his lashes like water through reeds. Then he smiled broadly at her and said, 'I had no idea today was going to turn out so well.'

She stifled a derisive snort and got to her feet again. 'I'm going,' she sighed.

But he stood up himself and looked down at her. 'You're staying. Aubrey was right. You *are* quite exceptional. The contract stands.'

She shook her head. 'I didn't show you my work in order to secure the commission, just to prove my point. Having done that, I'm leaving. You can consider yourself free to sue whoever you like.'

'You like the idea of standing up in court and telling the whole world all about us, do you? You do surprise me, Rosie. I'm amazed you didn't go for a swift and sensational divorce hearing, in that case.'

Rosie flinched. He had caught her on a raw nerve. Of course she didn't want to have anything made public about their marriage. She had her pride. She didn't want her humiliation and hurt planted out like a municipal flowerbed for the public's entertainment.

'I don't object to your suing Aubrey over a simple clause in a business contract, if that's how it has to be. It's hardly the sort of stuff the gossip columnists go wild for.'

'How little you know...' he murmured softly. 'Aubrey will have to contest matters, show some justification for varying the terms of the contract. Or at least he will if I'm not simply to ride roughshod over him and take him for every penny he has. Just exactly how good an old family friend is your Mr Greenslade?'

Not that good, thought Rosie bleakly. She kept her chin high and met his eye, but she couldn't think of a damn thing to say.

He bent to close her portfolio. 'Come on,' he urged. 'Start picking up those tiles. I thought you were in a hurry to be on your way?'

'You wouldn't really do that, would you?' she asked uncertainly.

He threw her a sardonic smile over his shoulder. 'There's only one way to find out...'

She pinched the edge of her lower lip between the middle finger and thumb of one hand. 'You wouldn't,' she said nervously. She was almost sure he wouldn't. After all, he was the one who'd behaved so despicably. He could have gone for an early divorce too. But he hadn't. He had far more to lose than she did if ever things came out in the open. Hellec Quebec Estates Ltd was a very high-profile company these days. It wasn't just Jack's reputation that was at stake. His share values would take something of a hammering, too.

'You wouldn't,' she repeated more confidently.

But he just raised one eyebrow quizzically and said nothing.

There was a long silence during which Rosie's emotions and thoughts performed acrobatics while Jack's blue eyes surveyed her levelly. 'Damn you!' she exclaimed fiercely at last. 'Get those wretched drawings back out. It seems we have a few business matters to discuss before I leave after all.'

He stood up, stretched and smiled. 'A perfect day,' he murmured. 'Quite, quite perfect...'

Ignore him. Ignore the man. Just think of him as a client. Be professional. That was the answer. And whatever you do, *don't* give in to the urge to cry. Don't. Not in any circumstances...

'I'm afraid the light isn't very good in here.' She glanced upwards at the dusty chandelier, whose electric candles pulsed out a faint yellow light. 'Is there somewhere with a better light where I can show you my work in more detail, Mr Hellec?'

'Jack,' he said with a cheerful insistence.

She raised her chin defiantly. 'I'd prefer to keep things on a business footing, Mr Hellec.'

'As you wish, Mrs Hellec.'

'No!' The word was out of her mouth before she'd had time to think. Her face coloured smartly. Damn him. He'd just won that argument very neatly.

'Ah! that's better,' he said insinuatingly. 'A blush! That's the Rosie I knew and——'

'And singularly failed to love!' she finished snappily, glad now that she was blushing. It saved her the trouble of having to do it all over again.

'You were the one who walked out, Rosie,' he said coldly. 'Or don't you remember?'

'Oh, I remember, Jack. I'll never forget the moment when I realised that whatever I thought you felt for me was a sham... So don't make out that you're the injured party.'

Hurriedly, before he could comment on her bitter
remark, she walked across to the French doors and
looked out. Beyond there was a loggia, the lichen-
speckled flagstones bathed in the amber light of the fine
autumn morning. There was also a white wrought-iron
table and chairs. 'Out there...' she said brusquely.
'Daylight is perfect.'

He came to stand beside her, withdrew a bunch of
keys from his trouser pocket, and with a deft movement
of the wrist shook out the appropriate key. He leaned
across her to insert it in the lock. Rosie lowered her eyes,
afraid that they might betray her. As he'd closed on her
she had caught the faint citrus tang of his aftershave and
the flame had leapt and flickered in her blood again. Of
all things, this urgent physical response was the very last
thing she would have expected. He had courted and
married her for the sake of another woman. Her own
sister. He had even made love to her for her sister's sake.
Just thinking of it nearly choked her with unutterable
distress. Yet still it was there: that hammering; that flut-
tering; that pulsing charge of desire.

The worst of it was that he'd positively enjoyed the
whole business. Once or twice in a darkened room he
might have convinced his inexperienced bride that duty
was the same thing as desire. But it hadn't been like that.
Not at all. Jack had wanted her, all right... Even while
he loved Emma. Loved her so much that he was prepared to degrade and humiliate a nineteen-year-old girl
on her behalf.

Jack had carried all of her bits and pieces out to the
table on the loggia. He had opened the portfolio and
was studying some photographs.

'I see what Aubrey meant about the tiles,' he said.

'Er—oh, yes.' She dragged her mind away from the
past and tried to concentrate on what Jack was saying.
She shouldn't have let her mind run on like that.

Thinking of it filled the flesh of her face with lead. Even her eyelids seemed heavy, as if she could only keep them open by a great effort of will.

He started to ask technical questions. She responded in a grey monochrome, none of her usual enthusiasm for her pet project surfacing to colour her words.

'Rosie, what *is* the matter with you?'

The curt irritability of his voice shocked her. How dared he speak to her like that after... after everything? Oh, how dared he? Anger flared like a bright flame.

'You're not serious? I mean, you can't really be puzzled can you, Jack? What's the *matter* with me? Can't you work it out?' she burst out incredulously.

It was Jack's turn to sigh. 'Are you really so unforgiving, Rosie? Hasn't time mellowed you at all?'

'Unforgiving? What sort of question is that, Jack? You deceived me in the worst possible way when I was very young and impressionable. I've changed since then. If I grew into an unforgiving person then you've only yourself to blame.'

She swallowed uncomfortably. It was a hard admission for her to make. She was by nature a very forgiving person. She wasn't contrived to relish the bitter taste of her own resentment. And yet she could not make it go away, although she knew that it was only herself who was tainted by it. She crossed to the table and began laying out the tiles neatly, concentrating on getting the corners matching precisely, although she wasn't usually so fastidious.

'I see.' He came to stand behind her. His hand reached out beside her own, taking tiles from the pile and spreading them casually beside her careful arrangement.

'Are you sure you haven't mellowed, Rosie?'

The words were spoken so close to her ear that she felt his breath warm on her cheek. She caught her lower lip between her teeth and nipped hard. His very presence

unnerved her. This proximity tested the very edges of
her self-control. 'I'm sure,' she said tightly. 'I can't imagine what you hope to gain from courting my forgiveness, if that's what you're doing. It can't be for the
sake of your conscience. You haven't got one. But
whatever it is you want, you're not going to get it from
me. Except good workmanship. I'm only here because
I don't want to make trouble for Aubrey.'

She glanced sideways at Jack. The hard planes of his
face were set grimly. He was standing with his hands in
his trouser pockets, staring down from the raised loggia
into the gentle sweep of the valley beyond. Sun-washed
cornfields, milky gold, patched the hills on the far side,
misty under the morning sun. It seemed too gentle a
landscape for his harsh gaze.

His voice when it came was damningly cold. 'Aubrey
stressed that you were particularly good at period work.
This place has been extended over the centuries . . . How
do you plan coping with that?'

'I—er——' She closed her dark eyes briefly. So that
was it? That was all those years had amounted to? A
brief conversation—quite polite in the circumstances—
and they were no more than business associates? *She*
had accounted for herself, while he—the man who had
planned to use her as a brood-mare—had given nothing
away. She might have known it. Rosie Wells might have
grown up, but she would never grow clever enough to
master a man like Jack Hellec.

Rosie began to outline the possible compromises while
he took her to see the lovely Jacobean house. He stood
close to her while he showed her around. It meant she
could feel the warm energy emanating from his body,
drawing it in with each small breath.

She had to continue standing close to him while he
showed her the kitchens and bathrooms, the pantry, the
old dairy and the thirty-year-old indoor pool, stained

and dusty from disuse, and then the endless succession
of fireplaces and hearths. The tiles were something which
she always undertook herself, rather than contracting
out. Modern tiles often changed the whole feel of an
older building, and she had developed an extraordinary
skill in making replica tiles, as well as decorating new
ones to create individual murals and borders.
Littlebourne Hall could have been purpose-built to eat
tiles. She had been hoping to be able to farm out as
much of the work as possible. But the tiles were going
to ensure that she would have to spend a disproportion-
ately large amount of time here at the house. Mournfully
she jotted down details, not able for one moment to enjoy
the idea of having such a splendid canvas for her work.

At length they found themselves in the suite of rooms
attached to the master bedroom. The bedroom itself was
enormous, commanding a view over the gentle vale from
a stone balcony beyond glass doors. The room boasted
a huge marble fireplace surround, though the grate itself
had been boarded up. Rosie knelt beside it, lifting the
edge of the carpet to see if the hearth had been left intact.

'Are you planning to reinstate the fireplace?' she
asked.

'Yes.'

'The surround is late Victorian. Do you want to keep
it, or restore the whole thing back to the original date
of the house?'

He shrugged. 'I think we should keep it. After all, the
bathroom is Victorian too, and I don't plan to do away
with that. The house has evolved over years with the
people who've inhabited it. It would be as much of a
travesty to destroy all their changes as it would to completely modernise it.'

Rosie couldn't help but agree, though she was increasingly longing to quarrel fiercely with him. The problem
was that her body didn't seem to have learned much over

the last four years. The more time she spent in his
presence, the more piercingly aware she was becoming
of him as a man. The heavy silk of her suit moved and
swayed, caressing limbs that already tingled with incipi-
ent sensuality. Luckily the drape of the jacket concealed
the fact that her breasts had hardened to tight points.

She wanted to roar with dismay, to run home and tear
off her clothes and subject her treacherous body to a
punishingly cold shower. Swathed in silk, she finally
understood the purpose of a hair shirt. She longed for
him to betray the cruel cast of his mind with his mouth.
To say something crass, objectionable, insensitive, so that
her flesh would recoil in tune with her mind.

But he didn't. The more he spoke of the house and
his response to it, the more reasonable and sensitive he
sounded. But then he always had. That had been the
problem. He had never betrayed by so much as a word
or a look the truth that she had been left to discover by
much crueller means.

Suddenly he gave her an unexpectedly direct look.
'You certainly know your stuff when it comes to houses,'
he said. 'It's hard to believe that your emotions haven't
matured at least a little...' His voice wasn't clipped and
businesslike now. It was like tar sucking over loose gravel.

She got to her feet swiftly. 'Are you trying to flatter
me into saying that I've forgiven you, Jack? Is that what
that little comment was all about?'

And then he came very close to her and laid one hand
on her shoulder.

'You haven't forgiven, Rosie. And I haven't forgotten.'

His fingers dug into her shoulder until she flinched.
She kept looking unseeingly straight ahead, trying to
ignore the thundering of her heart. His other hand came
up to her chin.

Sullenly, unresistingly, she allowed him to tilt her face towards his. 'Forgotten what, Jack?' she asked nastily, and then wished that she'd thought before she spoke.

Because, to her horror, it gave him the perfect opportunity to demonstrate just exactly what he meant. His head came down and his mouth brushed roughly against her own.

'That's part of the reason, Rosie. I haven't forgotten what it was like to kiss you. I wanted you then. And that much at least hasn't changed.'

She turned her head briskly to one side, biting frantically on both her lips in turn, desperately trying to erase the lingering sensation. But it could not be so easily achieved. Her whole body was throbbing with awareness . . . waiting . . .

'And Emma?' she asked desperately. 'Have you forgotten her?'

'*I* haven't, Rosie.'

So his relationship with her sister was still going on? And yet he could still bring his mouth down on hers like that . . . ? She ought to have been aghast. But nothing had changed. It hadn't stopped him kissing her all those years ago, either.

'Oh, you're hateful! Let me go!' she cried, shaking herself free of his biting grip.

'How far?' he asked drily. 'Across the room, or halfway across the country, never to return?'

'I shall keep on with the job. For Aubrey's sake, you understand. But don't you dare ever lay a finger on me again, or I'll have you prosecuted for assault.'

He gave a soft, dangerous laugh. 'Really? You're my wife still, Rosie. Or had you forgotten? It would be hard to make any accusation stick. But don't worry. I shan't let you go quite so easily this time.'

'You couldn't have done anything, *anything* to have made me stay then. And you can only push your threats so far this time, Jack. I'll do my work. But if you push me too far I'll call your bluff and walk out again.'

He shrugged. 'You certainly left in style then. Where did you go?'

Rosie clasped her trembling hands one inside the other. She had gone to Bristol to stay with a friend. An old schoolfriend with a big heart and a small flat, and the good sense not to ask too many questions.

'I want to leave now,' she said quietly. 'I shall bring some preliminary sketches with me when next we have to meet.'

'I want you here tomorrow at nine sharp. I shall have to be here to await a few calls. You can measure up or whatever it is you have to do while I'm working. We can have lunch.'

'I don't need to do that yet,' she protested. 'I have plenty to be getting on with in my own studio.'

He stared at her piercingly. 'Nine o'clock. Don't be difficult or I may have to look elsewhere for a designer, after all.'

She flashed him a fierce look. 'Then nine o'clock it will be...' she echoed scathingly, making for the door.

CHAPTER FOUR

'YOU'RE late.'

Jack was waiting for her when she pulled up on the large circle of driveway. He was standing on the top step in front of the massive front doors, his feet apart, his arms folded. The fabric of his navy suit was stretched taut across his shoulders.

'I'm not. Well, less than a minute and a half,' replied Rosie, glancing at her watch, then meeting his eye with a determined directness. She had chosen to wear a smoky-blue trouser suit today, with a short page-boy jacket and peg-topped trousers. It was beautifully tailored. She had selected it from her wardrobe in the hope that its austere lines would daunt him. But as she stepped out across the driveway and ascended the steps, her back straight, she realised that it had been a vain hope. Jack was not a man to be daunted.

'You look good with your hair up,' he commented crisply as she approached him, her head held high.

There was something in the way he spoke which told her that it was not intended to be a compliment. None the less she nodded a courteous acknowledgement.

'Good morning, Jack,' she said coolly. The worst was over. Nothing could be worse than yesterday. She felt quite prepared for anything he might throw at her today. But merely approaching him had set her nerves jangling. She had not yet managed to come to terms with the disturbing fact that she found him as attractive as ever.

53

'I haven't breakfasted yet,' he said, ignoring her greeting. A small frown line had carved itself between his straight eyebrows. 'You can join me.'

'I've eaten already,' she returned composedly.

He shrugged insolently. 'You don't need to eat. You need only sit.'

'What for? So that you can enjoy throwing a few more unpleasant remarks in my direction? Will it help your digestion?'

'So that we can discuss this damned house, assuming you still want the job,' he returned caustically.

Rosie lowered her dark eyes. She followed him submissively. How long was she going to have to endure his insistent dominance? A defiant anger was already stirring in the pit of her stomach and she'd only been with him for five minutes.

The breakfast-room was light and airy. He went to the sideboard and helped himself to devilled kidneys and a glass of fresh orange juice. Then he sat down and unfolded a copy of the *Financial Times*, which he proceeded to read as he ate. He paid her no attention at all.

The anger surged slightly, and then ebbed. There was no point in allowing herself to be riled by him. Hadn't he damaged her enough as it was? It wouldn't happen again. She would rise above it. She followed his lead, helping herself to a cup of coffee from a heavy silver pot. Then she quietly lowered herself into the chair directly across the rosewood table from where he sat, concealed by his paper.

Eventually he folded the paper neatly and set it beside his plate. 'Well?' he asked, his keen eyes narrowing, his face alert and attentive.

'Well what? You haven't exactly got the conversation off to a flying start so far.'

'That's supposed to be your job. You're supposed to be bubbling with creative ideas, aren't you? Or at least that's what I thought I was paying you for.'

'You haven't paid me a penny yet. And even when you do, I doubt I'll bubble. I don't effervesce in the company of rats.'

He raised his brows quizzically. 'So I'm a rat? Well, I guess that's your problem, not mine. You chose to marry a rat. I chose to marry a very beautiful young woman. Looked at from my point of view, I seem to have come out of the arrangement rather better than you, don't you think?'

Rosie hissed softly between her teeth. How on earth had he managed to turn the tables so deftly? 'At least,' she muttered coldly, 'I came out of the arrangement with my pride intact.'

'Well done.'

There was something unpleasantly dismissive in the way he spoke those two brief words. Now what had brought that on? She scowled in reply.

'Take your hair down, Rosie,' he said, looking at her dispassionately.

Her eyes widened with aggrieved surprise. 'What an extraordinary thing to ask!'

He didn't say anything. But he leaned back slightly in his chair and looked at her through narrowed eyes, those lines fanning out from the corners.

She was aware of his scrutiny. Too aware. She felt a hot blush crawl up her neck. 'Damn you,' she muttered.

He gave a brief laugh. 'Why are you blushing, Rosie?'

'I'm not blushing, I'm just getting angry. You're going too far. I'm leaving,' she said icily, pushing her chair back from the table.

'No,' he commanded. 'Stay here. I want to talk to you.'

She sat hard on the anger. 'I don't want to listen,' she countered.

'None the less...' He made a dismissive gesture, as if to imply that she had no choice. Then he leant across the table towards her, studying her intently. 'Unpin your hair,' he ordered again.

'What?'

'You heard me. Let your hair down. You look different with it up.'

'And you want always to remember me just as I was?' she commented sarcastically. 'How sweet.'

'Something like that.'

'Go to hell.'

At first when he got up from his chair she thought he was going to fetch himself some toast or a cup of coffee. But he came round behind her and unclipped the big tortoiseshell slide which held her hair in place. She had heavy hair. Very long. It dropped like a curtain around her shoulders and halfway down her back. Then he went and fetched himself some toast and a cup of coffee.

Meanwhile Rosie sat rigidly in her seat. She lifted her arms to the back of her head and began plaiting the nut-brown strands. By the time he had taken the first sip of his coffee she had it neatly back out of the way.

'Yesterday,' she said, her voice small with anger, 'I told you never to lay a finger on me again.'

'So you did,' he acknowledged calmly, breaking a corner off a piece of toast and smudging it with butter and marmalade. 'What was it you threatened me with? An assault charge?' He nodded towards the telephone on the sideboard. 'Feel free to make any calls you like. The number you require is, I believe, 999.' And then he put the piece of toast in his mouth.

Rosie's nostrils quivered with fury, not least because of the way he was eating his toast. He never buttered the whole slice, but broke off small bits until he'd eaten as much as he wanted. And she didn't want to remember the way in which he ate his breakfast. The way his angular jaw moved. The way the tip of his tongue came out to touch his lips now and again. She didn't want to remember anything about him. She looked down at her knotted hands. She studied her nails.

'Been gardening, Rosie?'

'I'm sorry...?'

'That first time I took you for a meal you kept looking at your hands like that. You'd noticed earth beneath your nails and were quite mortified. I almost called the waiter over to bring you a nailbrush on a silver salver. Remember?'

Of course she remembered! If she cared to, in the right mood, she could recall every single detail of that evening. She didn't like the idea that he should recall it, though. It gave him too much power.

'No,' she bit out.

'Did you go to university, after all?'

'No.'

'That's a shame. You should have done.'

She had jabbered on about her plans that evening. Later, after they had married, he had insisted that she should continue her studies. He had claimed they could be together in the long vacations, and that as he had to travel so much with his work it would be a good thing. She had thought it was delightful that he cared about the fact that she was so young... that there was so much she had still to do... like improving her mind, for goodness' sake! Huh! His only real interest in her mind had been in manipulating it. He had wanted her at university so that he could be free to spend time with Emma while she incubated his baby. She swallowed hard.

'I didn't continue with my education straight away,' she said briskly, anxious that he shouldn't guess that he had come very close to ruining her entire life on his account. 'I'd always been torn between the artistic and the academic side of my studies. I decided to take time out to consider my choice.'

The truth was that she'd hidden herself away as a clerk in a small insurance office in Bristol. It had been her father who'd encouraged her to study part-time at something creative, though even he hadn't been able to persuade her to apply for a full-time college course. All those students ready to take a genuine interest in her had somehow lost their appeal. Later, when she'd regained some of her lost confidence, she had attended courses in a local college and had finally picked up her diploma in interior design. She'd worked very successfully for a while with a large Bristol design consultancy before returning to Dorset just six months previously to set up in business on her own.

'Did you enjoy being a student?'

'Of course.' Not of course. At first she had hated going to her classes, wary of the attention of the male students, afraid to trust her own judgement even over matters like colours and textures. Gradually she had opened out, and learned to be happy again. She still hadn't liked the male students too much, though. When she dated them she'd found them . . . well, too young and unformed, thin and watery almost, insubstantial. After Jack.

'And then?'

'Then I set up a studio at home. I was lucky right from the start. Aubrey took an interest and put some work my way—and another friend of my father's— Marguerite. She has a furniture shop in Dorchester. It's a clever mixture of antiques and some of the best new Scandinavian stuff. She was looking out for someone to replicate broken tiles on wash-stands and fireplaces and so on. I did a little work for her. Now she does an awful lot for me. I expect I'll be using her when it comes to refurbishing some of the rooms here. Anyway, it just sort of took off.'

There was a pause in the conversation while he chewed a mouthful of toast.

Rosie steeled herself. The conversation had lost its cutting edge. He seemed quite relaxed now—not as if he was about to start challenging her again. She folded her arms and surveyed him. Over the years he had become a monster in her mind. And yet, despite the decisive ruthlessness of his manner, she was far less cowed by him than she would have expected herself to be. When it came to work she knew she was going to be able to cope with him without any problems. He was straight-forward. He would say what he thought. And she was even beginning to admire his taste. It was the personal side of their relationship which alarmed her. Because she couldn't ignore the fact that his physical presence affected her relentlessly. When he'd brushed his lips against hers the previous day she ought to have been absolutely disgusted. Instead she had craved more...

'How's Emma?' She asked the question deliberately to provoke that disgust. A reminder of his love for her sister should go a long way to switching off her automatic responses.

He stopped chewing. His face was impassive. But somewhere behind his eyes she sensed a lightening, as if the mere mention of her name had pleased him. 'I scarcely see her these days. Maybe once or twice a year—sometimes only for a few hours when I'm in New York on business. She's working out there.'

So he hadn't set up home with the woman who was unable to provide him with a son and heir? And yet he couldn't break things off with her completely, either...

'Will she be coming here to Littlebourne?'

'That,' he said coolly, 'rather depends.'

'On what?'

'On you, of course.'

'You mean I have a choice?'

'Yes.'

Rosie glared at him. 'Well, it makes a change. In that case I'd rather you confined your meetings to Manhattan.'

His eyes flickered a cold acquiescence. The light had gone.

Rosie drove the grimace off her face. She had already decided that he had bought Littlebourne so that Emma could try her hand at winning their father's love all for herself, too. But it looked as if she had been wrong about that. She was relieved. It wasn't that she feared losing her father's loyalty—that could never happen. But she was desperately afraid that one day her father would learn exactly how badly his elder daughter had turned out. Whenever he spoke of Emma it was with a father's love and affection colouring his words. More than ever she felt the need to shield the big man who had protected *her* so generously all her life.

So what was going on? Why had Jack bought this house? She sighed. Did it matter, anyway? She wasn't going to get dragged into any of his nasty schemes this time round, whatever they might be. And yet despite everything she still felt unreasonably glad that he saw so little of her sister. And it wasn't her head or her heart which had quickened at the news... It was that blind pulse, deep inside, which beat only for him.

She kept her eyes on her hands, afraid of finding herself watching him across the table...watching him and waiting. She felt a lump gather in her throat as she remembered how innocently she had once relished watching him eat, while her body learned to wait...

At last Jack put an elbow on the table and cupped his chin in his hand, staring at her. 'You should have left your hair loose,' he said.

Well! Comments like that had their uses. They were very effective at dispersing lumps in the throat, for instance.

'I thought we were supposed to be discussing work,' she returned waspishly.

'Ah, yes. So we were. Tell me about the pool, Rosie. Do you have any special plans for it?'

'Yes. I'd like to fill it with water and push you in.'

He gave a dry smile.

'Preferably after having hit you over the head with a blunt instrument.'

His smile broadened.

She didn't want him to smile. It did things to his eyes, his face, which she'd rather not remember. She switched tack. 'Actually, I do have an idea for the pool. There's a painting by Seurat... *The Bathers*... Do you know it? It's so full of light and air and it captures the feeling of people bathing on a fine day so perfectly... Well, I don't want to copy it or do a pastiche or anything but I just keep thinking of it as a sort of starting-point. The atmosphere. You know. That technique of applying colour in tiny dots, for instance, so that the whole surface seems to hum... Colour on ceramics is so pure—once it's been fired it retains its vibrancy—it doesn't discolour or anything. I thought of creating great clouds of light— of sun and mist and landscapes, hot and tempting...' She tailed off, glancing across at him.

His face was serious, alert once more. 'Go on,' he said curtly.

'Well, that's it, really. I haven't got any further than that.'

He shrugged. 'I know the painting you mean. Yes, it sounds good. Keep working on it.'

She felt mildly pleased, not least because they were, at last, talking about work. Encouraged, she heaved a sigh of relief and continued, 'And the dairy... I've had a really good idea about that. Well, I think it's good, but of course it's up to you. It's your house, and you have the final say. But I'm afraid I'm really struck by my plans for the dairy... If you don't like them I'll definitely be disappointed. I'll probably inflict them on my next client, regardless of whether or not they're suitable! They'll end up with a painting of a cheese on their toilet wall or something. Anyway, to get back to the point, you know those old-fashioned butcher's shops——'

But whatever he might or might not have known about old-fashioned butcher's shops was never to be revealed. He pushed his chair sharply back from the table while she was in mid-flow, and got to his feet, a tense vehemence marshalling his movements. She thought, fleetingly, that he was going to come near to her once more and... well, maybe let her hair down again or something. But he walked directly towards the door.

'Tell me some other time,' he cut in coldly. 'I've got business of my own to attend to. I'll see you at twelve for lunch. OK?'

Rosie was left sitting, mouth agape, feeling distinctly unnerved. Why had he got up and left so abruptly? She sensed strongly that it was something she'd said—and yet she'd said nothing of consequence at all.

The housekeeper came just after midday to remind her that she was expected in the drawing-room. She had been investigating the fireplaces, hoping to get all the tile work out of the way as soon as possible.

He was waiting there, looking out through the French windows across the loggia to the sweeping gardens beyond. A log fire burned merrily in the grate. Rosie ensconced herself in a Regency-striped Queen Anne chair to one side of the fire and said nothing.

'What will you have to drink?' he asked, turning from the window and crossing the large room.

She kept her eyes glued on the flames. 'Oh...'

But before she could organise her reply he had burst out laughing. 'What on earth have you been doing?' he asked.

Rosie hastily glanced down at herself. Her dauntingly austere trouser suit was patched with dusty marks. She slapped ineffectually at the trousers.

'I've been measuring the fireplaces,' she returned.

'You've got a smut on your nose,' he smiled.

She extracted a tissue from her bag and scrubbed at it.

'Now it's all red...' he commented.

'Well,' she said archly, her eyes glittering, 'so we've established that you aren't colour-blind? That should make my job a little easier. I'll have a tonic water. With ice and lemon, thank you.'

Jack laughed roundly. And then he said, 'Tonic water. Ah...yes. So that you don't sleep the afternoon away, I take it? Alcohol at lunchtime can have that effect on some people...especially if they aren't used to having their nocturnal rest disturbed...'

Darker than pitch. More viscous than molasses. Low and seductive, nudging at the dark cloisters of her memory. Rosie pushed stray wisps of hair back from her face with a flurried gesture, and looked back into the fire. She didn't answer. After all, it wasn't really a question.

On the day after the wedding they had drunk oodles of champagne at lunchtime after a night spent making love. Rosie had taken a walk to clear her head, and had been found by Jack, two hours later, asleep on one of London's numerous park benches. He had carried her back to their hotel room, while she had at first protested, and then giggled, and then snuggled close against his shoulders and... She wriggled uncomfortably in her high-necked jacket. The fire was really much too hot.

He handed her the drink, then came to sit in the chair opposite, stretching out his legs in front of the fire. 'I love fires...' he said. 'What do you plan to do with the hearth in this room?'

Rosie looked frankly into his eyes. 'Board it up. I'll look around for a second-hand fan heater.'

His eyes were dark with amusement as they met hers. He smiled. 'You wouldn't dare,' he said matter-of-factly.

'No,' she agreed. 'It would be pointless. You have to OK everything first so I couldn't get away with a stunt like that, much as I'd like to. And anyway, I enjoy my work too much to spoil things on your account. You aren't worth it.'

His gaze didn't falter. But the corners of his mouth curved gently upwards. 'Supposing I waived my right to veto your designs? Suppose I gave you *carte blanche* to do whatever you wanted with the house?'

'Like sell it to an ordinary couple with two-point-four children and their hearts in the right places? The sort of people I might really enjoy having as neighbours?'

'Like decorate it entirely according to your own taste...'

'That would be fantastic,' she replied. 'I'd love it. The clients are the main problem with my job. Unfortunately one has to accommodate their ideas. And given that you're such a big problem anyway, and that the very idea of doing anything to please you makes me feel quite ill, I can't think of anything I'd like better than being relieved of that particular obligation.'

He tilted his head slightly to one side. 'OK, then. It's a deal. You are to decorate the house exactly as you would if it were your own. Except for the poolhouse. I've been thinking——'

'Excuse me, but I think I've just developed a fault with my reception... Did you really say that I could do what I wanted?'

'Not exactly. I said you were free to decorate the house as if it were your own. Given that you've already indicated that you want to deprive me of my fireplace, not to mention my home, I don't think I'd better go so far as to let you do exactly as you want—yet. Anyway, to get back to the poolhouse——'

'But why?'

He shrugged. 'Why not? I'm busy. I've seen enough of your work to know that you won't let me down. And Aubrey certainly thinks very highly of you...'

Rosie was about to beam with pleasure, but caught herself in time. She really mustn't let herself be seduced for one moment by those guileless blue eyes of his. She viewed him suspiciously. She would do well to remember that this man had once deceived her quite unscrupulously. He was perfectly capable of doing the same again. But try as she might she couldn't see why he should make an offer like that in order to trick her. What would be the point? Perhaps she should take it all at face value? He did have quite a business empire to attend to, after all...

'Stop squinting at me,' he said, narrowing his own eyes, 'and listen while I explain about the pool. I think Aubrey mentioned to me that you already know about the hotels?'

'He said something, yes. But I don't really understand. I thought Hellec Quebec were involved in large-scale industrial development? Or have you decided that the time has come to make a career move into chambermaiding?'

'Are you *quite* incapable of sticking to the point?'

'Yes. I always have been. Remember?' And then she nearly bit off her tongue as she registered his slow smile of recognition. It was bad enough when *he* reminded *her* of those shared weeks. Now she was doing it herself. That damned tongue of hers!

'I'm diversifying. Hellec Quebec is a very large company these days. I determine policy, but I've a good team who undertake all the day-to-day decisions for me. Apart from the financial advantages of diversifying, I rather like the idea of embarking upon a smaller project in which I can be more personally involved. So I've bought up some dilapidated country houses to convert. Each one will have a swimming-pool and health club attached. That idea you had for tiling the poolhouse has really captured my imagination. I'd like to look into the possibility of devising a theme for the sports facilities based on your idea which will be common to all the hotels. I'll take you up to London to talk it over with Aubrey as soon as you've knocked your ideas into shape.'

'No, you won't.'

'And why not?'

'You're not taking me anywhere. I shall drive myself to London if need be.'

'I shan't pay expenses.'

Rosie shrugged. 'I think Chrysalis can afford to finance the trip.'

'And if I decide to relocate the meeting to Milan?'

Rosie proffered a withering look. 'Forget it, Jack. I don't know what you're up to, but whatever it is it won't work.'

'Won't it?' he said softly.

There he was, smiling again. His lips were pressed together in a straight line, but his eyes were glinting behind the dark hedge of lashes and those little lines were there at the corners again. Rosie squirmed in her seat. That pulse had started up, deep inside, flickering in time to the volley of his voice. Try as she might she couldn't dispel this nightmarish consciousness of his body, stretched out, relaxed, in the chair opposite her own.

During lunch Jack turned on the charm. It was a weird experience, watching him treat her with such polished grace. Rosie leaned back from the table for most of the meal, regarding him warily as he proceeded to compliment both her work and her person.

At last, over the fresh raspberries and cream, she decided to call a halt.

'Why don't you just spell it out, Jack? You want something from me. Last time I was fool enough to be taken in by you. It's not going to happen twice. You could save yourself a lot of trouble by just telling me.'

One corner of his mouth tilted obliquely. 'Now why should you think that?'

'Because you're a devious, conniving rat.'

'And you are . . . ?'

'Compared to you I'm a timid little country mouse.'

He pursed his lips assessingly. Lines of amusement carved themselves into his face. It made him heart-rendingly attractive. She looked resolutely over his shoulder.

'Do you like the house?' he asked.

'You're not answering my question.'

'No. But nor have you answered mine.'

'OK. So it's a beautiful house. I used to come here as a child, actually. We knew the family who lived here then. I've always liked it.'

'I know.'

Rosie flinched. Emma, of course. It pained her to think how much he might already know about her. Whereas she knew next to nothing about him. Given the natural tendency of her tongue she'd done more than her fair share of the talking in those long-gone days. He had the edge, whichever way you looked at it.

'Why did you buy it?'

'I liked it too.'

'Oh, come on! You're not trying to tell me that it's sheer coincidence that you moved in just a couple of miles from me?'

'No.'

Horrified, Rosie felt herself colouring again. She'd been the one to ask him to tell her the truth, and now that the conversation was veering in that direction she was finding it harder to take than she'd imagined. She dipped her head, wishing that she'd left her hair loose after all.

'Then why?' she persisted, determined, despite her own discomfort, not to let him off the hook.

He lifted his shoulders casually. 'Oh, it was far enough away from London for the area not to be besieged by commuters. I liked the idea of making the acquaintance of my neighbours. I figured the local people around here might prove very interesting.'

'That's just a roundabout way of saying that you moved here to meddle in my life in some way, isn't it?' she returned accusingly.

'Yes.'

Damn him. She had never seen anyone squirm less. Let him off the hook? He'd never been on it in the first place!

'Well,' she exclaimed crossly, 'I hope the house makes you very happy! Because I can assure you that this particular neighbour won't.'

'I'm always happy, Rosie,' he said laconically. 'Especially now...'

'Liar,' she muttered.

'Oh, no. I shall get what I came here for. I'm sure of that.'

Determinedly she shook her head.

'Are *you* happy, Rosie?' he asked when she failed to come up with a comment.

She twisted a tendril of hair away from her face. 'Extremely,' she snapped.

'Liar...' he returned in tones so soft and treacly that the fine hairs on the back of her neck stood on end.

She frowned at him, her annoyance abruptly giving way to dismay at her own response. 'Naturally, I don't exactly feel like dancing for joy in your presence. But I can assure you that I shall when I finally get away from here. And generally I couldn't be more content with my life.'

'Contentment isn't happiness.'

She looked up. 'Contentment is everything when you've tasted the alternatives, Jack,' she said quietly, speaking at last a deeply felt truth. She smoothed a few stray wisps of hair back from her face.

'You've calmed down. You aren't angry any more,' he commented, tilting his head as he watched her.

'What makes you say that?'

'Those strands of hair that keep wafting across your face? They're your weather-vane, Rosie. When you blow them away you're feeling cheerful. You smooth them back when you're in a contemplative mood. And you twist them around your index finger and make little corkscrews of them when you're annoyed.'

'That can't possibly be true,' she said haughtily. 'After all, my hands are at this moment neatly folded in my lap. If what you said was right I'd be practically knitting socks with my hair right now.'

He shook his head. 'No. You aren't angry with me. Not really. And you haven't been, by and large, since you came down for lunch. I take it as an excellent sign. As I said, I couldn't be happier.'

Rosie pushed her dish away from her, meeting his eye. 'Can I return the favour, Jack? Can I tell you what your most revealing feature is?'

'Be my guest.' He regarded her with a disarming openness.

She wasn't about to be fooled. 'It's your eyes, Jack. You've trained them to give nothing away—to lie on your behalf. Before I discovered that, I found them utterly deceiving. Now that I know, I can use them to read you like a book. When your eyes practically melt with sincerity, I can be certain that you're lying through your teeth.'

He laughed again, a laugh which seemed to resound with genuine amusement. None of it meant anything, Rosie reminded herself disdainfully. None of it. He wasn't really happy to be with her. He wasn't really diverted by the things she said. He probably didn't even like her designs very much. Rosie felt slightly sick. All this table-talk was beginning to repel her.

As soon as she'd taken the obligatory few sips of coffee she got up to leave, insisting that she had an appointment to keep.

Jack's eyes narrowed. Languidly he got to his feet. 'I'll just see you to the door.'

To her surprise as soon as they were through the door he took her firmly by the elbow and marched her into the huge oak-panelled hall. 'I'll pick you up about seven,' he said briskly with an engaging smile. 'OK?'

She was quite taken aback. 'Absolutely not OK. My evenings are my own.'

'No, they're not. I'm taking you out for dinner.'

Rosie shook her head calmly. 'No, Jack,' she repeated insistently.

But he merely caught hold of her other elbow too and looked down into her eyes. 'I still want you, Rosie,' he said. His voice was cloud-soft and dangerous—as were his eyes. 'Despite everything I still want you. So I shall begin wooing you all over again. Starting tonight.'

Rosie's heart was beginning to hammer wildly inside her chest. Facing him like this, so close to him, with his hands gripping her arms, his eyes threatening hers so sweetly, she felt a rash of desire creep from the small of her back, across her shoulders to her nape.

'No,' she insisted, shakily.

To her dismay he loosed one elbow, and used his free hand to unfasten the slide which once again was holding her hair into a heavy twist at the back of her head. It fell, and he combed it through with his fingers, settling it over her shoulders, around her face. The tips of his fingers brushed against the honeyed skin of her cheek. She shivered, shrinking away from him, her eyes still held by his.

'No...' she said more firmly.

'My God, Rosie,' he murmured drily, 'it's still there for you too, isn't it? You can feel it, can't you?'

'I don't know what you mean,' she muttered tightly.

It was the wrong thing to have said. His mouth curled into a cynical smile. 'Really?' he asked. And then he pulled her close to him. He didn't kiss her, though. He simply held her against his long, lean frame. 'Surely,' he said softly, 'you can feel it now?' And he took one of her hands and crushed it between them, against his chest. Which meant, unfortunately, that his wrist pressed close against her breast, calling from it a charge of excitement so strong that it scalded her.

She twisted her head to one side, struggling to free herself. Abruptly he let her go. She stepped backwards sharply.

'Stop playing these games, Jack,' she said through clenched teeth.

'It's not a game, Rosie,' he said softly.

'Jack, you don't really want *me*. You can't.'

'Oh, but I do.'

'Well, you're wasting your time. You won't succeed.'

'Really?'

'No.'

'Why didn't you tell your father about our marriage?'

Rosie tossed her head and met his eye coldly. 'It hardly seemed sufficiently important to bother mentioning it.'

'Oh, Rosie, that's not the truth, and you know it...'

She glared furiously at him. 'Why bother to ask if you know so much?'

'Seven,' he said again, turning to go.

'No...' she said woodenly, but he was already walking away. If he had heard, he didn't acknowledge it.

CHAPTER FIVE

MARGUERITE dropped by late that afternoon, patting her auburn curls and smoothing down her pencil-slim red skirt as she wriggled out of her boisterous old sports car. Rosie had known her for years, and despite the age-difference they had become firm friends in the months since her return. Marguerite had a warm heart and a good sense of humour as well as a rather heavy hand with the mascara wand. She also had an ex-husband—about whom the least said the better—and an avowed desire to replace him with something more fitting. Her standards, though, as Rosie had mutely observed, were impossibly high. Despite her claims that anything with a fat wallet and a civil tongue would do, she was, in reality, notoriously hard to please. There were plenty of suitors, all with smiles as healthy as their bank balances. But they never lasted long. Rosie wished that she and her father would hurry up in realising that they generated sparks from each other. For such intelligent people they could be awfully dense at times.

'Tea or coffee, Marguerite?'

The older woman stood up and patted her flat tummy even flatter. 'Coffee. Black, no sugar. I'm back on my diet.'

'What's his name?' grinned Rosie, setting out a pair of earthenware mugs.

Marguerite crushed her heavily painted lips together in a wry smile. 'Am I really that obvious?'

'Yes.'

She shrugged. 'His name's Jack Hellec, he's stunning, and he's bought Littlebourne. Oh, and he's not attached.'

Rosie felt the smile tighten on her face. 'Er—actually, I've met him. I'm decorating the old place for him. I was going to mention it. There'll be a lot of work coming your way too, I expect.'

'Oh, Lord. You mean he's set eyes on you already? Then I may as well have sugar after all. Though, on second thoughts, maybe he prefers the more mature type... It's not unknown...' Marguerite threw back her head and gave one of her throaty chuckles. 'In fact there's something about your expression that tells me I'm welcome to him. What's the matter, Rosie?'

'Shut up, Marguerite.'

'Certainly, my dear. Now where's your father's coffee? I'll pop it down to him if you're busy.'

'You know perfectly well that he has a kettle in the stables. And he hates being interrupted when he's working.'

'But we're old friends, Rosie... He won't mind.'

'Hmm. You know quite well that he'll mind. He'll bawl you out for breaking his concentration. Face up to it, Marguerite. You want to see the man himself at any price.'

The laugh this time rattled the cups on the dresser. Nature had bestowed upon Marguerite the most resounding belly-laugh ever to be found in a female of the species. It was quite at odds with her polished appearance, as she was only too aware. She saved it for friends. 'Don't be silly. You know I'm not interested in courting your dear papa.'

'I can't see why not. He's smashing.'

'But married, my dear, to that ghastly sweater of his. He won't do, I'm afraid. The search must go on.'

Rosie grinned. Life couldn't be all bad when there were people like Marguerite walking the face of the earth. At least it had its entertainment value.

Their banter persisted until Danny Wells appeared, his beard thick with stone dust and his eyes disgruntled behind floury lashes.

'Work not going well, Dad?'

'Horrible. I'm working on a very voluptuous lady, and I can't seem to get her curves in the right places.'

Marguerite sucked in her cheeks and her tummy at the same time. The action had the effect of thrusting her decidedly curvaceous bosom into increased prominence. 'I'd offer to model, but my figure is too positively *gaunt* to be of any use, I'm afraid.'

Danny blinked disbelievingly. 'The power of positive thinking, eh, Marguerite?' he said laconically. 'Back on your diet, no doubt. What's his name?'

Marguerite growled.

Rosie slipped unobtrusively out of the kitchen. She didn't much want to hear the rest of the conversation— especially the bit where Jack Hellec's name was prised from Marguerite's strawberry-crushed lips. She certainly didn't want to be around to answer any awkward questions.

She took a quick shower, then padded down to the sitting-room to keep watch on the front door. If Jack was going to turn up as promised she wanted to be on hand to answer the door and dispatch him before either Marguerite or her father got a whiff of his presence. His big black car pulled into the driveway at six minutes past seven.

'Go and get dressed,' he said when she had opened it a crack, precipitating his knock.

'I've already eaten,' she lied defiantly.

'We've had this conversation once today already. And the answer's the same. You don't need to eat. All you need to do is sit.'

'No. Not even that.'

'OK. Stand, then. But you're coming.'

'I'm not.'

He folded his arms and stood looking at her as she glowered back at him. He stuck one foot between the jamb and the door. 'Hurry up.'

'No.' She even pushed on the door, but it didn't close. Nor did his eyes register anything. Like pain, for instance.

'Is your father in?' he asked coolly. 'I'd like to meet him.'

'No,' she spat. She dared not risk their meeting. Her father would naturally ask questions, and then, inevitably, it would all come out. The truth would break his heart. 'Go and sit in your car,' she said resignedly. 'I'll get changed. I'll be with you in five minutes.'

He smiled his acquiescence, then sauntered towards the car. She waited until he was behind the wheel, the door closed, before she hurried upstairs, tearing off her sweatshirt and unzipping her jeans as she went.

She flung herself into the passenger seat of the car in record time. Over the stuffy aura of the expensively trimmed interior she could sense the redolence of his body. She opened her window wide. But his presence refused to be diluted by the fresh air. He was inescapable.

'Good,' he said. 'Five minutes. That's exactly how long it took you to get into a dress last time. It seems you understand the rules already.'

She looked sideways at him. 'Last time,' she said coldly, 'I dressed quickly because I was anxious not to keep you waiting. I was infatuated with you then. Tonight is quite different. I don't want to be here. I merely want to get the evening over with as quickly as possible.'

He started the engine and let in the gears. 'You looked sweet in that white dress,' he said softly, easing the car out into the narrow country road. 'Your taste in clothes has changed. It's good. Sharper. Cooler. Like you.'

Rosie glanced down at her dress. It was deceptively simple, made from a buttercup-yellow crêpe. It was a hard colour to wear, but looked marvellous against her honey-coloured skin and dark eyes. The bodice was bias-cut with cap sleeves and the skirt draped elegantly to mid-calf level. Her only accessories were a pair of flat petrel-blue ballerina shoes and a matching soft leather belt. It was true, she knew, that she had developed an unerring eye for the wholesome lines of good, well-designed clothes.

Perhaps she *was* sharper and cooler, after all? She was certainly proud of her womanliness. The white broderie anglaise had told the world that she was a girl—an *ingénue*. She had not worn that dress again—nor one like it—since Jack had made love to her on their wedding day. And yet, no matter what protest her clothes might make, there had never been another man since Jack. Not really. Woman she might be, but woman alone she had remained.

As if reading her thoughts, he said, 'There's no man in your life, Rosie?'

'Not at present, no.' There wasn't any point in lying.

'Not since me,' he said flatly, his eyes fixed to the road.

'I... Honestly... What on earth makes you say that?'

He turned his head fleetingly and gave her a sardonic smile. 'An old schoolfriend of Emma's said something a few months ago... Her brother invited you out, apparently. It set me wondering. And then when I held you today... I knew.'

'You couldn't be more wrong,' she protested, chokingly. But he just ignored her, the smile still on his face.

'Do you still garden, Rosie?' he asked at length.

'Can we talk about the house, please?' she sighed wearily.

'No,' he replied, with a surprising smile. 'You didn't know you were going to become a designer that first night. We never mentioned wallpaper so much as once.'

Rosie gave a bitter laugh. 'You mean we have to replicate our original conversation, word for word? Is that the game we're playing?'

'No. I mean that we can talk about anything and nothing. Just as we did that night. It wasn't what we said that was important, anyway. It was all the things we wanted to say but held back, wasn't it, Rosie?'

She turned her head to look out of the window. It was dusk. The landscape was gathering into violet and grey strands. 'Was it?' she muttered in an offhand voice.

'You know it was. And tonight it will be the same. We'll sit and eat dinner, and I'll look at you and you'll look at me, and we can fancy each other like mad all over again.'

'I hate you,' she responded heavily.

He shrugged. 'As I said,' he murmured, 'it's not what we say that matters tonight. The words are meaningless, which is why we can't talk business. We'd have to concentrate too much on the words if we did. After all, it wasn't business that brought us together that evening...'

Rosie's mouth tightened with hurt. 'That's a lie. *You* were there on business, Jack. It wasn't a chance meeting for *you*.'

She glanced sourly at him. The comment had bitten home. Even in the dusky light she could see the darkening of his skin, the savage thrust of his jaw which followed her remark.

He was silent for the remainder of the drive. His mood had altered once again by the time they arrived at the hotel. The same hotel. He was civilised and charming, just as he had been at lunchtime, and all those times before. And he was right. They talked about this and that over the meal, but what they said was unimportant. It was the way his mouth moved forming the words, the way he filled the space across the table, the way her skin sensed his presence and craved the brush of his hand as he seated her which echoed in her mind. Despite herself, the game was being played. Rosie wanted to lay her head on the damask cloth and weep for the futility of it all. There could be no pleasure in playing a game which you knew you would never win.

Stiffly she asked questions and gave replies with none of the excitement which had made her gabble and laugh and bite at her lip at this same table, four years before. The only relief the evening afforded came right at the end when he dropped her back at her home, and, just as then, refrained from kissing her. He hadn't needed to. She already felt plundered—despoiled—by the strength of her own response. One kiss could have made no difference.

A few days later he rang and asked her to come over to the Hall to look at some pieces of furniture he was having delivered from London, to see how they might be incorporated.

'But Marguerite is the expert. Couldn't you get her to come and see them?'

'*You* make the decisions, not her,' he said emphatically.

He was right, of course. It was a valid enough request. She had to go.

'Come and see the gardens,' he said, before she was out of the car.

'You want them decorated? Fine. It's unusual, but I think I can manage it.'

'I'd like your opinion, certainly.' He proffered a sultry look from under his straight brows.

Now what on earth was that look supposed to signify? This persistent charm of his was irritating her beyond belief, mainly because, when he was being civilised and pleasant and looked at her like that, she was more than ever aware of his potent sexuality. It seemed to seethe about him at such times, a tangible presence in the air between them. But a fraudulent presence. When he was brusque with her he was at least being honest. She was attracted to him then too, but she could cope with that. It was just her own crazy instinct dancing its own infuriating jig. But when he provided music, in the form of smiles and compliments and sultry looks, she hated herself for her response. She felt used then, and angry at her weakness in succumbing. She forced herself to ignore him. She didn't quibble about going with him to see the gardens, though. She was beginning to realise that there was little point.

The grounds ran to some thirty or forty acres. 'I'll tile it. But we're talking big money, Jack,' she commented crisply. 'Earth-moving equipment, hard core, scree—my fortune will be made, yours lost.'

'Stop talking about tiles. Tell me what you really want to do with it.'

'Why do you ask?'

'It will be your garden one day. I want to know what you want. After all, you're something of an expert. You must have some ideas.'

So the question was part of his self-confessed courtship ritual? Rosie narrowed her eyes thoughtfully. 'Well, put like that it's very tempting ... yes ...'

She grinned. 'I think a factory on the parkland over there—you know, one of those box-like factories in a brilliant blue. And there, where the copse is, perhaps a maximum-security prison, with high walls all around. A motorway link across the formal gardens... A fire station in the orchard... A cement works on the lawns——'

'Seriously.'

'Seriously, I'd like it to be someone else's garden. Why don't you move?'

'You're all sweetness and light, Rosie.'

'Aren't I? It's nice that you're beginning to appreciate my finer points at last, Jack.'

'Come on. Wouldn't you like to have all this to play with? Kitchen gardens, herb gardens... You could do what you wanted.'

Rosie surveyed the rolling parkland in front of her. 'Hmm... Yes, the idea does have potential. A maze perhaps, to lose you in. Poison ivy, nettles, deadly nightshade, hemlock, monk's-hood... Those sort of alterations might have quite an appealing practical application as well as being ecologically sound. But you're wasting your time if you think I can be bought with a few bedding plants and a packet of seeds... My soul doesn't come so cheap.'

'Did I say I thought you could be bought?'

'No. But that was the implication. Jump into my bed and I'll let you have a go with my daisy dibber.'

'You're underestimating me.'

'Oh, no, Jack! Whatever gave you that idea? I could never underestimate you. My opinion of you is rock-bottom as it is. It couldn't possibly sink any lower.'

'So being mistress of all you survey doesn't tempt you?'

'Not when *you're* in my sight-lines, no. Anyway, you're forgetting, I have a delightful garden of my own.'

'It's not your own.'

'OK, technically it's my father's. But to all intents and purposes it's mine.'

'But surely you'd like to get away?'

'Jack, remind me to buy you a history book—one that gives the dates of the Dark Ages. The days when women married simply to escape the family home are long gone.'

'I wasn't suggesting you come to me in order to escape your home. I was simply pointing out that when we do get back together all this garden will be yours. More properly yours than is your father's.'

'I'm quite happy, tending his patch. I can't imagine why you should think I'm not.'

He raised his eyebrows, as if to throw doubt on the veracity of her last statement. But he didn't comment. Instead he said, 'The removal men called to say the van had broken down. The furniture hasn't arrived.'

'Then why didn't you ring and tell me?' she sighed, aggrieved. 'Oh, don't bother to answer. I won't like your reply. Now if you'll excuse me I'll get back to some serious work . . .'

But Jack said firmly, 'No, you won't. You didn't think I'd let you come all the way out here just to go back home? We're going sailing.'

Rosie groaned and rolled her eyes. 'You're wasting——'

'Stop it!' His voice grated like a saw-blade on stone. 'I'm tired of your protestations. You're every bit as attracted to me as ever you were. You are coming out for a couple of hours in my boat. We will talk about jibs and booms and painters, and we will get very cold. We will not rake over the past. I will not lay a finger on you. But when you go home later you will have something to think about. Right?'

She pulled a wry face, but she didn't waste her breath contradicting him. Let him drive her to Weymouth. Let him take her out in that little boat of his again. It had been fun crewing for him the last time. This time it would be awful, cramped into the small boat with him, too close to him, confined, breathing him in with the raw salt air, craving him. But there would be no real temptation. There was nothing to fear. Her body could hum all it liked, but she'd *never* dance to its tune.

The little yacht had been traded for something a good deal larger. With a crew.

'You've been working hard these past years,' she said with grudging admiration as she climbed on board.

'I have concentrated *entirely* on work, these past years,' he said meaningfully.

But it was the only meaningful thing they said all afternoon. They talked about jibs and booms and painters, and drank tea while they leaned over the rail and looked at the grey slap of the chilly sea, and, afterwards, in a quayside pub, drank a glass of beer and looked at the jumble of boats and masts and cottages beyond the window. When they returned to the car he turned on the heater full blast. He'd been right. She had got very cold. And she did have a lot to think about. Like the fact that she'd enjoyed his company.

He'd said that they would leave the past behind, and that was exactly what had happened. Her insides had lurched every time she turned her head and saw him profiled against the sky. And she had kept on and on looking. She hadn't turned away, sick with self-loathing, while they floated away into the grey continuum of sky and sea. She shoved her clenched fists into the pockets of her jeans. She *had* been tempted, after all. And now she was very frightened indeed.

He spent the next week in London. She worked frenziedly for the whole week, hoping to get as much under her belt as possible while he was away. She saw Marguerite two or three times during the interval, but dodged any mention of Jack.

At last Marguerite turned to her impatiently and said, 'Honestly, Rosie, it's not all going to go away just because you don't talk about it.'

'What isn't going to go away?'

'I don't know. You tell me. There's obviously something very powerful going on between the pair of you, but I haven't a clue what it's all about.'

'Haven't you?' muttered Rosie, suddenly suspicious. Marguerite had spent a whole afternoon at Littlebourne. And Marguerite, on form, could draw confidences from a house-fly in half an hour. Anyway, Jack was up to something. It might have suited him very well to have a friend of Rosie's all agog. 'Jack's said something to you, hasn't he?'

Marguerite gave a loud shout of laughter. 'Yes. He has said something as a matter of fact.'

'What did he say?'

'Ah-ha! That would be telling...'

Rosie shook her head, frustratedly. 'You don't understand him. He's terribly devious. He's manipulating you...'

'No, he's not.'

'How can you say that when he's told you a pack of lies about me and him and what happened...?'

'But he hasn't. He said...wait a minute...' and her fuchsia lips moved while she counted on her fingers '...nine words. That's all. It hardly constituted the story of your life.'

'Nine words? What were they?'

'I'm not telling you. Though I wish you'd tell me what it's all about. You two have met before, haven't you?'

'Shut up, Marguerite.'

'OK. But he can't make you do anything you don't want to do, Rosie. You can call your own shots, you know. I'll back you a hundred per cent if you need it. You know that.' Marguerite gave her a sympathetic smile

at that juncture. 'I wouldn't get so het up about him if
I were you. After all, he's putting so much business your
way... If I were you I'd just forget all the personal stuff,
do the work, and wait to become rich and famous on
the strength of it. Huh?'

It sounded eminently reasonable, put like that. It
sounded anything but when Jack turned up on a misty
Sunday morning, wearing cords and a cream sweater instead of a suit. Rosie was raking leaves from the grass
under the beech trees when he appeared.

'Put that down and come with me,' he demanded,
surveying her with folded arms.

She looked at him over her shoulder, red-faced from
exertion, strands of her hair trailing around her shoulders
and neck where they had worked loose from the thick
plait.

'Go away,' she replied furiously. The jolt of seeing
him had made her press down sharply on the rake, and
now the prongs were imprisoned in the heavy soil. She
jiggled angrily at it, tearing at the turf.

He came and took it from her, and eased it neatly out
of the ground. Then he laid it upon the grass. 'Come
on,' he said.

'I told you to go away,' she said haughtily, pulling her
shoulders back and twisting a strand of hair away from
her face.

He smiled. 'Come along. We're going for a walk,' and
he caught hold of her arm.

She shook him off disdainfully, but he simply slung
an arm around her shoulder and began to walk anyway.
She could have kept her feet resolutely fixed to the spot,
but that would have meant stumbling against him.
Reluctantly she moved.

'Jack, I don't want to——'

He ignored her. 'Last time you were delighted to see me,' he reminded her. 'You said you knew I'd come back and we——'

'Shut up. I don't know how you have the gall to remind me. What I said four years ago was said in all honesty—unlike all the things *you* said.'

'Not all, Rosie.'

She looked across at him in pained disgust. 'Don't split hairs. You came here under false pretences. And you're here under false pretences this time as well. Emma and you are up to something again, aren't you?'

'Not Emma. Just me. When I learned you'd moved back here I decided it was time I bought myself a country house and came to find you.'

'Oh, really? So that you could resurrect the love-affair of the century, huh? It won't wash, Jack. Why don't you just go away?'

He was leading her down towards the lake. 'I'm not going,' he said unequivocally. 'Is the punt still going strong?'

She dodged out from under the weight of his arm then and glared at him. 'My God! You're not planning another little ride in the punt, are you? What exactly do you have in mind? Another proposal of marriage, or will you just satisfy yourself with seducing me?'

His blue eyes were cold. 'Neither,' he said, a precarious anger underlining the word. 'I don't need to bother with either. We're still married, Rosie. And I don't intend making love with you until you're ready for it. Which, sooner or later, you will be.'

'Never!'

But his arm was back across her back, and he was leading her forcefully towards the water. 'You're lying to yourself, Rosie,' he said. 'You still want me. Nothing has changed. Except that this time we both know the

score. You won't fight me forever. You'll be prepared
to forget the past soon. Just as I am.'

'How noble of you! So you're prepared to forget how
abysmally you treated me...?' Her sarcasm bravely
masked her mounting fear. She couldn't cope much
longer. She was bone-weary of rejecting him when her
skin was so hungry for him. Every time she was with
him the battle became more terrible. Of course, reason
would prevail in the end. Of course. It had to, didn't it?
If she yielded to him it would mean that she had no
pride; no self-respect; that she was nothing but a craven
victim of her animal senses... She would never give
herself up to that, would she?

His face hardened into grim lines. 'OK. So I treated
you badly. But your behaviour has never been exactly
above reproach. I have to admit I hadn't counted on
your still being so incredibly bitter. It's not the most attractive of traits. But I'm prepared to overlook it.'

She hit him then. She landed a furious punch squarely
on his ribs and began pummelling at him with all her
might. His fingers held her shoulders, while he took it
all unflinchingly, his face set. When the fury ebbed and
her arms fell limply to her sides he pulled her roughly
against him and began to kiss her.

She held her mouth fast closed against the onslaught
of his. But the hot scent of him in her nostrils could not
be repulsed. Desire erupted fiercely inside her. It was as
if all the moments they had spent in each other's presence
since he came to Dorset had been fuelling her need. A
thick, powerful column of arousal roared up through
her, so that she pressed her thighs tight together in a
futile attempt to quell it.

His tongue probed against the fullness of her closed
lips, but she would not give way. And then his hand
came up and cupped her breast through the soft cotton
jersey of her sweatshirt. His thumb found the nipple,

and swiftly circled its betraying hardness. The sensation pierced her with its sweetness, so that her lips parted minutely in response. His tongue penetrated their moist guard, powerfully exploring the world beyond. She was helpless. She opened her mouth to him then and let him kiss her with a hard urgency. Passively she stood, her face uplifted to his, her heart desperately angry, her body aching with delight. One hand ran down her back, coming to rest lightly on her jeans-clad bottom. He pulled her towards him so that she felt his arousal hard against her. The shocking intimacy of the gesture jolted her senses back into life, so that she dragged free of his arms.

'I hate you!' she cried, her teeth clenched. 'And I hate myself for letting you do that. You can forget the contract—everything. Just go away!'

He looked at her with a strange intensity, then laughed. 'Didn't I tell you that you'd give in, in the end? It didn't take long, did it, Rosie?' And with a burst of energy he strode to the water's edge, calling cheerfully over his shoulder, 'Where's the punt?'

She paused just long enough to point it out. 'There!' she said bitterly, gesturing towards a muddle of rushes and dead leaves some way along the bank. And then she turned and ran back to the house, leaving him to discover the sodden craft, mossy and leaking, for himself. She glanced back over her shoulder as she ran. The leaves on the lime trees had turned, thick yellow against the creamy sky. Smoke hung in the air as poignant as a dream. He was crouching at the water's edge, one hand caressing the blackened wood, his gaze turned outwards to the grey and gold mirror of the lake. It had been an autumn day such as this when she had set the old punt adrift to meet its fate. For four years now she had watched it decay, longing only for the day when it would sink without trace.

He found her in her studio. He meandered through the door, his sleeves pushed back to reveal the smooth dark hairs which covered his forearms, his hands shoved nonchalantly into his trouser pockets. Her head was bent to the drawing-board, a pencil in her shaking hand.

'I'll pick you up at about eight tomorrow morning,' he said. 'Bring all the stuff for the pool tiles. We're lunching with Aubrey.'

She sucked on her lower lip before replying. 'I'm not coming. I told you. The whole thing's off. I don't care any more. You can tell Aubrey what you like.'

'You'd better pack a case for a few days. Three, four...I'm not sure. It depends how long it takes. I couldn't take you out in the punt, but I'm looking forward to taking you to London again.'

She kept her eyes on the blank sheet of paper in front of her. 'You won't get me into bed in three or four days. In fact, you won't achieve it in a lifetime. The deal is off.'

He gave a brief laugh. 'No, it's not. We've gone too far...'

She closed her eyes. 'Are you referring to the kiss or the work? If it's the kiss, then I have to agree. We went way too far. It won't happen again. As far as the work is concerned, we're only a couple of weeks into it. You can easily find someone else.'

'Are you refusing point-blank to have any more to do with the Hall?'

'Yes.'

He inclined his head gravely, the corners of his mouth tugging downwards. 'Perhaps I'll postpone the meeting after all. Marguerite's invited me to join your father and herself for a meal tomorrow... I'd rather like to meet him, as it happens...'

She looked at him then, swivelling on her stool to search out his eyes. Her own were dark with fear. 'You wouldn't?'

'I damn well would,' he assured her, a faint smile beginning to play around his firmly modelled lips.

The hard resolution of his clear blue eyes provided all the convincing she needed. She turned slowly back to the board, folded her arms upon it and laid down her head.

'Eight o'clock,' she murmured faintly, her voice whispering out across the blank sheet of paper. 'One portfolio. One suitcase. I'll be waiting. And I think you stink.'

He came and lifted a lock of moist hair from her cheek, and looked down into the dead darkness of her eyes. 'Why did you wreck the punt?' he asked.

'Why do you think?' she asked lifelessly.

He dropped the strand of hair back on to her cheek as if it were a venomous insect, and walked away.

CHAPTER SIX

JACK arrived promptly at eight. Rosie was waiting on
the steps, dressed neatly in a forest-green skirt and jacket
with a high-necked white blouse, her suitcase and portfolio at the ready. He handed her in before loading her
luggage into the back. He scarcely looked at her until
he had restarted the engine and was ready to move. Then
he turned his head and gave her a long, assessing look.

'You look bloody awful,' he said, tersely, then edged
the car out on to the road.

Rosie didn't bother to reply. She was not looking
forward to the next few days at all, and saw no reason
why she should bother to disguise her feelings.

'Too pale. You're not usually pale. What's the matter?
Are you feeling ill or something?'

'I didn't sleep well,' she responded coldly, through dry
lips. 'Guess why?'

This time he was the one to remain silent. She stared
ahead out of the windscreen, but was none the less conscious of his head turning time and again in her direction.

To her surprise, when he next spoke it was to tell her
about his plans for the hotels. Eventually he won her
interest sufficiently for her to throw in an occasional
question. Rosie soon found herself relaxing into the
blessedly neutral conversation. It wasn't until the car
began to weave its way through the outskirts of London
that her old apprehension returned.

'Where are you taking me?' she asked.

'Where would you like to go?'

'Who cares? Everywhere is equally grim with you by my side.'

'These conversations are so dreary. Surely you must realise that all your protestations are a waste of time.'

She breathed deeply before allowing herself to reply. He was wrong. He must be. And yet on the boat she had been tempted by the man himself. And down by the lake she had been tempted by his kiss. Put the two together and she was a lost cause... Disdainfully she said, 'Is that what you think? That you're bound to get your own way? That if you persist, like water dripping on a stone, you'll wear me down in the end?'

'No. I think that sooner or later you'll realise we can have something good together. You do still want me, Rosie. I have to admit when you packed your bags I had my doubts. But you were lying then. If I didn't believe that I wouldn't be with you now. It's been a long time. I didn't expect it to be easy. But you remember how it was, too. And you'll come to me in the end.'

'You're making a big mistake. I'm an immovable object. You, however, as far as I am concerned, are anything but an irresistible force.'

He gave a dry laugh. 'I'm not planning on using either force or mere persistence to prove my point. Because you're not the immovable object you like to think you are. I moved you yesterday, down by the lake.'

'A hair's breadth. What you're looking for would require an earthquake.'

'Then I shall build us a house on the San Andreas fault and await developments there.'

Rosie gave him a withering look, but his eyes were fixed on the road.

'You still haven't told me where you're taking me.'

'Haven't I?' He paused, then added, 'London.'

She groaned. 'Where will we be staying, though? Because if you've got any crumby ideas about taking me back to that hotel...'

'You're right.'

'You mean we are going there! Then let me tell you——'

'No. I mean you're right that it would be a crumby idea to go back to that particular hotel. It's been taken over by a multinational chain who guarantee the same characterless room in any one of forty-six countries worldwide. Not quite what we were used to, eh?'

'So where——?'

'Wait and see. Anyway, we've got business to attend to first. We're having lunch with Aubrey and there's a lot of planning to do...'

Thank goodness for Aubrey. At least she had a few hours' grace before the torment began.

Aubrey Greenslade was a handsome man in his fifties, with thick white hair and a humorous smile. He enveloped Rosie in a bear-hug as soon as she walked into the room.

'I'm always tempted to say how much you've grown, Rosie. You still look like that cheeky little girl who pelted me with rotten plums...'

'Aubrey, do you have to remind me of that every single time we meet? And anyway, it served you right for getting Dad that commission in Amsterdam. He'd promised to take me fishing. You ruined a perfect day. If you will go around finding work for happily unemployed sculptors and turning them back into bad-tempered working artists, you must learn to live with the consequences. Actually, I had an even better idea than the plums, but the bees weren't in a co-operative mood that day.'

Aubrey grinned. 'How are you getting on with our Rosie, Jack?' he asked, his eyes twinkling. 'Does her conversation drive you mad? It's lucky for us she has such a lively mind—at least when she disgorges its contents it's a pleasure to listen. Imagine if she carried on like that about the merits of different brands of washing powder?'

Jack was unnaturally silent. He was staring coolly into the middle distance. He didn't look as if he was considering his reply. In fact, he rather looked as if he hadn't even heard the question.

Rosie hastily cuffed Aubrey on the arm and embarked on her own reply, embarrassed by Jack's refusal to respond. She didn't want Aubrey to suspect anything. 'Huh! You can be quite an old windbag yourself when you get stuck into a bottle of port. It would serve you right if I spent the next hour telling you exactly what I think about a whole variety of domestic products. In fact I might just do that...starting with—er—ammonia and working my way right through the alphabet to—er—ah—Zebrite.'

'Zebrite?' queried Jack drily.

So he *was* following the conversation after all...? Rosie raised her brows humorously. 'I haven't made it up,' she said primly. 'It's a brand of grate polish. Like blacklead. Actually, it's fantastic stuff. When we get some of those fireplaces of yours buffed up with it you'll——'

'Rosie!' roared Aubrey. 'For goodness' sake stop it! I take it all back. You're the most economical conversationalist in the world. Positively terse, my dear.'

Rosie grimaced, but the older man had already turned his attention to her portfolio. He was extremely impressed by the designs, and took Rosie's arm companionably on the way to the restaurant. They continued to josh each other amiably throughout the meal, while Jack urbanely turned the conversation back to business whenever it threatened to stray too far.

'Aubrey,' said Jack at length, pushing his plate to one side, 'I'm thinking of setting up a small factory under Rosie's control, so that she can cope with the quantities of tiles we'll need. She's a one-man band at present. She'll need skilled help. But something like that will need to be a long-term venture. What do you think?'

'Good idea,' nodded Aubrey. 'Essential, in fact. And if it works well I think our firm can promise to put a fair bit of work her way for a long time to come.'

Rosie frowned. 'Wait a minute,' she said. 'This is the first I've heard of any of this...'

Jack shrugged insouciantly. 'You haven't got much choice, Rosie. The pool alone is going to mean thousands of tiles. If you paint them all yourself it will take months. We haven't got that long...'

'No, but I'd already made plans for subcontracting——'

'Jack's right,' interrupted Aubrey. 'You can't do it all yourself. And once the factory's up and running you'll be able to handle all sorts of major commissions.' He smiled warmly, turning to Jack. 'She gets her talent from her father, you know. Tremendous man, Danny. Brilliant sculptor. Wonderful sense of humour too. The man can make a cat laugh, especially when he's had a few beers. Does he still lunch at the Farmer's Arms, Rosie? The locals all think the world of him, Jack.'

Jack looked hard into Aubrey's eyes. 'Oddly enough,' he said softly, 'I've never met Rosie's father.' He paused, then added, his voice dark and insinuating. 'Perhaps it's time that I did.'

Rosie's ran her tongue across her lips. The last thing she wanted was Jack and her father exchanging anecdotes over a pint.

'He's very busy at the moment,' she said evenly. 'He's working on a major piece. He hates to be disturbed.'

'Maybe I could catch him one lunch-hour...' said Jack, his voice treacly.

Rosie offered him a weak smile, her eyes narrow and hard. 'You think he'd like that, do you?' she said as sweetly as she could manage.

'I think I would,' returned Jack, meeting her cold gaze.

'My father,' she said softly, 'chooses his own friends. And he's very picky.'

Aubrey had obviously sensed the undercurrent. 'This,' he boomed affably, 'is not getting the baby bathed, Jack. If we go back to my office you can look over the new computer visualisations, and I'll go through Rosie's portfolio more carefully, and have a chat with her about this factory idea.'

Rosie heaved a sigh of relief. But Jack shook his head. 'Not this afternoon, Aubrey. I have a couple of other appointments.'

A brief look of puzzled dismay ran across Aubrey's features. Clearly he'd been expecting a long session with Jack. But Jack had already got to his feet, a determined air about him, and with a charming smile was holding Rosie's jacket ready for her. Rosie remained seated, looking over her shoulder at Jack with an equally determined expression in her eyes.

'I—er—if it's all right with Aubrey I'd be terribly interested——'

'Didn't I mention the appointments earlier, Rosie? How careless of me. I'm afraid I shall need you with me,' and his hand went controllingly to her elbow.

Rosie was torn for a moment. She supposed she could make a fuss. But a quick look at Aubrey warned her that it would be pointless. He was smiling warmly at Jack, obviously anxious to please such an important client.

'Absolutely. Absolutely. You run along, my dear. Now he comes to mention it I do recall Jack saying something earlier... Stupid of me to have forgotten...'

With a small shrug of angry resignation Rosie got to her feet and snatched her jacket from Jack. He might be leading her by the nose, but she was damned if she was going to simper while he held out her jacket for her. She could at least dress herself.

Once out in the street she turned on him. 'What on earth was all that about? There aren't any other appointments, are there?'

'No.'

'Then why did you want to get me away from Aubrey? Because we get on well together? Surely you didn't think I was giving him a come-on or anything, did you? Honestly——'

'No. I didn't think that.'

'Then why?'

'Drop it.'

'I don't understand you, Jack. I know you're cunning. But at times you act so oddly. We were getting on famously. Work was being discussed in a reasonable manner, and then...pmmmph! Off you go. It's like that time you made me watch you eat breakfast. You just cut out then, in the same sort of way. I figured that this time round I would be able to understand what you were up to. But I'm like one of those poor laboratory rats in a maze, and I don't mind admitting it. There's something—well, random, in the way you behave with me. You've got me beat.'

He kept on walking, not turning his head to look at her.

Good. She didn't like him to look at her. 'I don't know what you've got planned for me. All this stuff about a factory, for instance. Wouldn't it have been good manners to have told me in the car on the way up, instead of springing it on me like that?'

'Yes. But I'm not terribly interested in good manners, you know.'

'Surprisingly, that's one of the things I *had* managed to figure out about you. But you haven't answered my question.'

'Why did I spring the idea on you in front of Aubrey? So you'd be forced to acquiesce, of course. You'd have turned the idea down flat otherwise, wouldn't you, for no sensible reason except that it came from me?'

'Not necessarily.' She paused for a moment. 'Well, actually I probably would have.'

'You can't do all this work alone, you know.'

'I realise that. In fact I'd already started making plans of my own. I could have sorted——'

'I know. But I'd rather sort it out for you.'

'Why? What makes you want to meddle in my life like that?'

'You really do have the shortest of memories, Rosie. We're married. I'm your husband. What could be more natural than——?'

'Oh, shut up.'

'Don't you want to know more about your new enterprise, Rosie?'

'I'll make the decisions myself, thank you.'

'Too late. I've acquired the premises and short-listed the applicants already...'

'What? This is unbelievable! You must be crazy. I won't have anything to do with your arrangements.'

'You will.'

'What makes you think you can make me?'

'My track record to date. So far you have insisted on a number of things. No breakfast. No loose hair. No dinner. No work. No kiss. Shall I continue?'

'I hate you.'

'So you keep saying. But I don't believe you.'

'Why not?'

'Because of this.' And right in the middle of central London, with people on every side, he grabbed hold of her and pressed his mouth to hers.

Great, Rosie found herself thinking with glee. He'd picked the wrong moment for once. She kicked out at his shins very hard, and when his mouth flew back in shock she shouted, 'Help! Help!'

Central London? The wrong moment? Jack? All those damned people and not one of them—*not one*—so much as turned a hair. Except Jack. He threw back his head and laughed. And then he started to walk again.

Rosie was ready to scream with frustration. This was the most incredible situation she had ever been in in all her life. She stood still, her knuckles white, her lips warm with desire, and watched Jack's broad shoulders receding in front of her. Aubrey... Marguerite... Her father... They would be appalled if they had so much as an inkling of what she was having to endure. All she had to do was to tell them the truth. OK, it would damage her pride. But she was being pushed further and further, and every moment she spent in his presence was making her more frightened. She wanted him. Very much. He was right. Sooner or later she would cave in and give herself to him, and what price her pride then?

The balance had changed. It would be far less humiliating now to pour it all out than to find herself shackled to him by lust. Her father would be badly hurt to think that she hadn't told him the whole truth sooner. And even more badly hurt, of course, when he discovered Emma's role in it all. But it was more than seven years now since he had seen her. Emma was twenty-five. A grown woman. He would hate to think that Rosie had lost her own self-respect to protect his memories of a child who had long gone.

She would give Jack a final chance to back off, to sell Littlebourne and get out of her life. If he refused then she would tell her father everything. She began to run, weaving her way past the people on the pavements, watching the back of his dark head as it moved onwards, inches taller than the crowd.

'Jack...' she gasped breathlessly.

'Darling!' he exclaimed drily. 'You're throwing yourself into my arms at last. I knew it could only be a matter of time——'

'Be quiet. I've got something I want to tell you.'

'Good. I'm all ears. Just wait till we're inside. It'll be a little more private there, don't you think?' And with that he extracted a bunch of keys from his pocket and took the wide steps to the impressive Georgian house in front of them, two at a time. He even managed to get the key in the lock and turn it. What game was he playing now? This wasn't a hotel...

Rosie looked around in bewilderment. She had thought they were wandering aimlessly. 'This is Harley Street,' she protested.

'That's right,' agreed Jack, opening the door.

'What are we doing here? Are you feeling ill?'

He smiled sardonically. 'Not all the houses in the street are consulting-rooms, you know. They're very fine houses. I've admired them for a long time. So I bought one. When I'm not in the country, this is where I live. Welcome to your town house, Mrs Hellec.'

Rosie's eyes widened in surprise. 'I'm not coming in,' she asserted. 'I'll talk to you out here on the street. But if you think——'

'Save your breath, Rosie,' he groaned. 'You know it makes sense,' and with a couple of strides he was back at her side and had picked her up and was heading back up the steps with her.

'Stop!'

'Don't bother to scream. Even if anyone takes any notice I've only to tell them that these are the premises of a top psychiatrist...'

She didn't bother to scream. As he had said, there was no point. They were over the threshold anyway by then and he'd kicked the door shut and deposited her on the thick blue carpet. Instead she sighed noisily.

Jack was smiling at her, his blue eyes dancing. 'That was nicely symbolic, wasn't it? Carrying you over the threshold like that.'

'I've already told you that you'll never get me to bed. So why you're continuing this farce about pretending we're married I don't know.'

'Because we are.'

'Not for much longer,' she said grimly, feeling wildly triumphant. 'Either you sell Littlebourne and clear off or I shall divorce you just as soon as I can. I shall tell the whole story in court, if need be. It will be as messy a divorce as you've ever witnessed. And I won't care one jot.' She paused. 'Now what do you think of that?'

He merely smiled in return, and began to lead the way up an imposing sweep of stairs. 'The drawing-room's upstairs. Why don't you join me in a glass of something? Now that the afternoon's appointments have been cancelled it seems like a rather appealing idea, don't you think?'

Rosie bit her lip. How on earth was she to make him take her seriously? She looked up at him. He was leaning over the curved mahogany banister rail, smiling at her. His straight brows had tilted slightly, and his upper lip bloomed blue above the smile.

'You aren't listening!' she exclaimed bitterly.

'I am. You're telling me all about this messy divorce you're planning to inflict on me. I simply thought I'd listen better with a drink in my hand. And you'll

probably tell it better with a drink in yours. Come on.'
And he took a few more steps up the stairs.

Rosie folded her arms. Now she had had time to take
in something of her surroundings she realised that this
really was a very grand house indeed, the sort of house
which was bound to be run by a small, unobtrusive staff.
She smiled.

'You go on up and pour yourself a drink, by all means.
Personally, I rather like this hallway. I think I'll stay
here to do my talking, if you don't mind. But don't
worry. I'll make every effort to make sure you can hear.'
And then she took a deep breath and shouted as loudly
as she could, 'I intend divorcing you. Very messily. I
shall make sure my father knows every detail about
Emma and you, in advance, and then I shall stand up
in court and spell it out for the benefit of anyone else
who may be interested.'

Jack hung over the banister again to look at her, this
time from a point near the top. He smiled broadly and
shouted back, 'What makes you think your father will
see it your way?'

She frowned up at him. 'Why shouldn't he?'

Jack tilted his head and continued to survey her. He
didn't look like a man who had just had the rug pulled
from under him. He looked pleased with himself.

'Don't you understand?' she roared angrily. 'It will
all come out in court! Everything!'

The contours of his mouth altered slightly, so that he
was smiling wryly. 'Only the bare bones need come out
unless I choose to contest it!'

For a second Rosie was completely nonplussed. But
her wits hadn't quite deserted her. She opened her mouth
wide and roared up the stairwell. 'Really? I thought that
if I were to sue you for a huge financial settlement it
might attract a fair bit of publicity whether you con-
tested it or not.'

'Do. I expect I'll be able to afford it.'

Suddenly her shout turned to a bellow as real anger caught hold of her voice. 'Damn you. Why won't you take me seriously?'

'Because,' said Jack, in a perfectly ordinary voice which sounded alarmingly quiet after all the shouting, 'I don't care what you say about me. In court, or anywhere else come to that. I did nothing to be ashamed of. I let you go because of the way *you* felt, and because you needed more time to grow up. Perhaps I shouldn't have married you in the first place... I don't know. All I knew then was that I'd fallen in love with you and I wanted you to be my wife.'

It was probably the only thing in the whole world that he could have said which was capable of reducing her to stunned silence. Bewildered, she began to mount the stairs.

CHAPTER SEVEN

THE drawing-room was huge, with big windows looking down on the bustle of the London street. There was a glowing coal fire in the Adam fireplace, and within seconds of her perching weakly on the edge of a sump-tuous chintz sofa a slim woman of around fifty in a neat grey dress had appeared with a bottle of champagne in an ice-bucket, complete with crystal flutes.

'Rosie, I'd like you to meet my housekeeper, Mrs Reeves. Mrs Reeves,' he said sombrely, 'this is my wife.'

Rosie attempted an embarrassed smile which the woman returned formally as she set the tray beside Jack. Then without a word she disappeared.

'A drink, Rosie?' suggested Jack with a cynical smile. She shook her head. 'Of course not.'

He looked at her reflectively. 'Won't you join me in my celebration? Come on. Even you must feel that I'm making excellent progress.' He picked up the bottle, and released the cork with a muffled pop.

'Progress to where? Hell? Yes, perhaps I might agree with you over that.'

'Come, come Rosie. Don't be so churlish. I've enticed you to London, and now you're ensnared in my drawing-room. I consider I'm doing exceptionally well.'

Why had he said he had loved her? Why? A huge ache was beginning to well up inside her. She was a fool. He'd only had to mention that particular four-letter word and she'd followed him upstairs as biddably as a dog. Nothing had changed, she reminded herself. She was as gullible as ever, while he could lie with his eyes alone. Lying through his teeth must be second nature to him.

'Ensnared me? When are you going to start treating me like a human being? That's when I shall consider that progress is being made.'

He crooked an eyebrow, sloshing some champagne into his glass. 'Are you sure you won't join me? Wine is for human beings, after all. Or perhaps you'd feel more comfortable nibbling on a piece of cheese?'

'You're making a bad mistake, Jack. I'm no mouse. I shall make sure that every last detail of your behaviour comes out in this divorce.'

He shrugged. 'I've told you, I don't care. Why should I? I should think you'd have more to fear from revealing everything than I do.'

A powerful memory of those torrid nights swept across her inner eye . . . He thought she was too timid to chance revealing anything of that? He was wrong. Her girlish features gave the impression, she supposed. But she was a woman now, and proud of it. She wouldn't relish the exposure, but she didn't fear it, either. They had been newly married. She had been very much in love. Why should she feel any shame?

'Why should I be afraid? I'm sure most people would consider that everything I did was quite natural in the circumstances.'

'Are you really so shameless, Rosie? Behind that pretty façade there's a heart of pure granite, isn't there? I doubt it even beats. It probably just gives off seismic waves.'

Her tongue clicked out a note of pure disgust. 'Still hoping for that earthquake?' she jeered caustically.

'Not hoping, no. I'm *expecting* it. You protest your scruples, but I don't believe in them. I doubt you'll hold out much longer.'

She looked furiously across the room at him. He was leaning back comfortably in his chair, the jacket of his grey suit unbuttoned, his long legs splayed. She had never seen anyone look less threatened in her entire life.

'I shall let you sue Aubrey, you know. I'll explain it all to him. He'll understand. And he'll weather it.'

At that point Jack stopped looking relaxed. He drew himself up in his seat, and plonked down his glass. Then he turned a deep-set pair of icy blue eyes on her and said disdainfully, 'So that's how far your loyalty to your friends extends? I might have known.'

He got restlessly to his feet and paced across to the window, his hands in his trouser pockets. He looked down on the street below, before muttering coldly, 'I don't know why I'm bothering with you. You're not worth it.'

Rosie knew she should have been glad that he seemed to be cooling off towards her. But she felt unaccountably dismayed. She wanted him to take seriously her threat to reveal the past. Implicit in it was a desire to make him acknowledge how badly he'd treated her. And yet, far from being concerned at the prospect, he'd treated the idea with equanimity. He seemed yet again to have turned the tables on her, and she couldn't understand why or how. He was making out that she was shameless—heartless—because she wasn't prepared to let him trample all over her for Aubrey's sake. And yet he was the one who was threatening to sue poor, innocent Aubrey, a well-respected professional man, nearing retirement, in order to make Rosie do what he wanted!

'Of course I don't want Aubrey to be dragged into this,' she muttered defensively. 'But you aren't giving me any choice. I don't want Aubrey hurt. And I don't want my father to know the whole truth either. But if it comes to a choice between that and being endlessly tormented by you, it's the option I'm prepared to take. And as for my being ashamed of my own part in it…well, you can take it from me that I'm not ashamed at all. In

fact, I don't think I have anything at all to regret. Except
that I allowed myself to be duped by you.'

'Your precious pride,' he said coldly.

'Yes,' she acknowledged bitterly. 'My pride is precious
to me. Now if you don't mind I shall be on my way.'

He turned to face her then, his gaze flinty. 'You're
staying, Rosie. You'll stay here in London with me until
I have turned back the hands of your emotional clock.'

'I'm going,' she insisted, making for the door.

But he stepped forward and detained her with just the
lightest of touches. Infuriatingly, her skin prickled wantonly at the gentle pressure of his hand on her shoulder.
Her nipples tightened into firm buds. Tears sprang to
her eyes as she realised how far she was from being able
to subdue this crushing need. She flinched visibly.

'This bickering isn't pleasant, is it, Rosie? If you go
now it will start up again the next time we're together.
I'm going to change things once and for all. By the finish
one of two things will have happened: either we'll be
man and wife together again, or I'll have decided that
I don't want you any more, after all.'

'You mean I can get to win, after all? I didn't realise
that prospect was open to me.'

'If I leave you won't have won, Rosie. You'll have lost
everything worth having. Your life will shrink and
shrivel. You'll stay bitter and sour forever. You'll nurse
your grievances till your dying day. It's no recipe for
happiness.'

'Oh, no...' she countered anxiously. 'I was fine before
you came back. I'll get there again.'

'Before I came back you didn't know how much you
still felt for me, Rosie. Now that you do the door is
shuttered and barred. Do you think you'll ever again
meet a man who can do this to you?' And he trailed his
fingers lingeringly across her breasts. She took a step
backwards, trembling.

'It's not everything,' she said in a choked voice.

He shrugged. 'No,' he agreed. 'It's not. But a life without it can be very empty. Especially for someone like you, Rosie. Will you meet another man, Rosie, and make love to him the way you did with me? Will you?'

'I could,' she insisted, hoping her voice wasn't betraying the uncertainty she felt in her heart. 'And anyway there are other things.'

'Like work? You have a job most people would envy. It offers rich rewards. Like mine. Do you think it's enough for you? You need more, Rosie... You can't change that.'

'There's self-respect,' she bit out fiercely. 'I don't know what the future holds for me. No one can know. But I can take on board whatever it offers with my head held high. That's surely as much as anyone can ask for.'

He ran his thumb from her temple, along her jaw to her chin. 'Is it?' That voice again—black as pitch.

'You're going to stay in London with me, Rosie,' he said mesmerically. 'You're going to find out exactly what the future may hold. If you leave I shall come and find you and bring you back. Last time when I let you go I thought it would only be for a short while. I thought you'd see that what you'd lost wasn't worth the price you were paying. And that you'd live a little and learn a little and then come back. But four years have gone by and you still haven't changed your mind.

'You're not a girl any more. You're a woman. And you've grown old enough to have forfeited the right to be allowed to grow up in your own way. The time has come for me to open your eyes for you—to make you see that your childish pride has outlived its usefulness. We're married, Rosie. We should be forging our future together. It's what you want whether you're prepared to face it or not. You can keep on fighting me. Keep on souring your mind with it all. Keep on with this bickering. But I'll do my damnedest to turn you around, you know. I'll make sure we resolve it in the end.'

'You mean I'll give in?'

He looked her up and down, then sighed. 'Maybe. Or you'll convince me that I don't want you after all. I have to admit that at the moment that seems the likelier outcome.'

She hesitated. She was surprised by his disdain. Was it all part of the game—designed to confuse her even further? Or did he mean it? There was only one way to find out.

She backed out from the taunting pressure of his hand, and perched herself on the edge of the sofa. 'Very well. I shall stay. I shall stay until you dislike me as much as I do you. Then perhaps you'll leave me alone and I can begin to get my life back together again. I'm quite ready to start the ball rolling. I have a great many things to say to you which I'm sure won't endear me to you at all. But before I begin to enumerate them I'd be grateful for a cup of tea. I'm thirsty—though unlike you I don't celebrate my rancour with champagne.'

Jack returned to his seat, and passed the message into an intercom at his side.

'Are you going to begin?' he asked contemptuously. 'Or will you wait for the tea to arrive?'

'I'll begin now if you like. Item one: I can't for the life of me understand how you can still be interested in constructing some sort of relationship with me when you're still seeing Emma. It beggars belief. I loathe you for it. Is that so very hard to understand?'

He gave a harsh laugh. 'It's not at all difficult to understand. And incidentally, you've started brilliantly. I do find it very off-putting to have you remind me of that little fact. At this rate I shall be walking out on you before the tea's even arrived.'

Rosie stared at him in bewilderment. 'Why does that particular criticism make you dislike me all the more? It should make you feel ashamed of yourself. Do you seriously expect me to ignore Emma? Am I breaking the rules by mentioning her?'

He sighed, looking coldly at her. 'I'd certainly rather concentrate on what we have between us, you and I, without dragging her name into it.'

'So what do we have, Jack? Apart from mutual contempt.'

'Mutual attraction.'

'Surely you can't be so very hard up for sex to allow that to sway you?'

'We once had love between us, Rosie. Not just sex.'

'You certainly never loved me.'

'Didn't I?'

'You turn my stomach. Remember, I heard what you and Emma said to one another. I know exactly how I was set up. If you call that love then you have a pretty paltry idea of what the word means.'

Jack just blinked and stared hard at the window. His face was a mask—but a hard mask. 'Do I?' he said softly.

'Anyway, whatever I felt for you changed the moment I saw you two together.'

'You said you hadn't loved me at all. That you were just curious to find out what it would be like to sleep with me.'

'I...I was in a terrible...' She tailed off, remembering the acrimonious words which had flown from her lips. 'That's right,' she said stiffly. 'Exactly. That's all it was. Curiosity.'

He looked piercingly into her eyes. 'Oh, don't lie to me now, Rosie. What's the point? For someone so sexually curious, so very passionate, you've led a remarkably staid life since then. Making love with me was special. You know that. And you cared for me until you

saw me with Emma. You said as much yourself not a
moment ago.'

She swallowed. 'OK,' she muttered thickly. Of all
things it pained her to admit as much to him. After all
the hurt he'd caused her she would have relished denying
it. But in all honesty she couldn't. 'But I stopped loving
you. I really did. And that's not going to change.' Her
chin was wrinkling ominously. Tears gathered behind her
eyes. She blinked them furiously away.

He screwed up his eyes for a moment, and then shoved
his hands into his pockets, almost angrily. 'How could
you just turn it off?'

Rosie attempted another shrug, but her shoulders were
trembling, and the gesture ended up stiff and awkward.
'Don't keep pretending, Jack. I heard what you said that
day. You know... About—er—about...' But her lips
were quivering and her voice was husky with emotion.
Any minute now she was going to burst into tears, no
matter how hard she fought it.

'About how happy I was with you?' he said in frozen
tones.

'No...' He hadn't said that! On the contrary... Oh,
he was lying as usual; she kept forgetting... 'No,' she
repeated. 'About how you and Emma were
planning... planning for me to...' But it was no good.
It was far, far too painful to talk about... She rubbed
one thumb jerkily back and forth along the line of her
brow, trying to soothe the turmoil inside her head. None
of it made sense.

'I...' Rosie swallowed hard. 'Jack, I don't understand. Why are you lying to me? Trying to pretend that
it was all... all right? That we loved each other and
everything. What are you trying to do to me? I thought
you simply wanted to resume our... our sexual relationship. I could, at least, understand that. But now

I'm lost . . . I thought that this time round I could handle everything, but I'm so confused and . . .'

Her voice began to shake badly as she spoke. And then she put her fingertips to her eyelids, and with an anxious, plucking motion she began to rub at the tears which were spilling unwelcome on to her cheeks.

Jack arrived at her side just moments before the silver teapot arrived in the room. Rosie swept tears away with her knuckles to flash the woman a brief smile of gratitude before covering her face with her hands and swallowing a muffled sob. Mrs Reeves discreetly slid out of the room, while Jack, seemingly oblivious to her presence, sank on to the arm of the sofa and gathered Rosie to him.

Her face was pressed against the fine linen of his shirt. She didn't want to pull back. All her resolution had drained away, leaving twisted and quaking emotion to take its place. She needed comforting. And, disturbingly, it was his comfort she wanted more than anything in the world. For long minutes she choked back tears while his hands soothed her shoulder-blades, lifting her hair away from her nape to stroke tenderly at the fine skin at the back of her neck, to curl his fingers gently amongst the wispy, baby-fine tendrils at her hairline.

She tasted the citrus tang of his aftershave in her mouth. She felt his heart thump steadily against her red, damp cheek. Her head was bowed, her fingers still rubbing convulsively at her eyes. She remembered with an aching sadness how it had been to love him—to trust him.

His mouth was against her hair, breathing calming endearments into its silky mass. She felt his breath scorch soft clouds against her scalp. Little by little the tears subsided, and the tortured muddle of thoughts melted away, leaving her mind empty and drained.

His mouth travelled to the high dome of her forehead, across its curve and down to the gently dipping bridge of her nose. His breath sang out across her hot, flushed cheeks and over the angle of her jaw. And then, delicately, like thistledown alighting on petals, his lips touched her own. The gesture was so restrained, so precise, that she felt no pressure from the coarse barb of his chin and upper lip. Just the firm, well-modelled lips, touching against the fullness of her own, side to side, rubbing, with a barely perceptible motion.

A noise halfway between a sob and a gasp shuddered in her throat. Her knotted hands relaxed, and one finger came, as if of its own accord, to touch his cheek. She felt the mysterious male roughness of his shaven skin prickle against her fingertip. And then, carried on a wave of mindless calm, the old desire began to seep, like oil, into every corner of her being. Her joints were fluid with it, her mind swam in it, her mouth was moist with it. She was in his arms, and she wanted him. Languorously her mouth began to open to his. Still his lips worked over hers with a light, fragile motion. Her willowy neck arched, her face tilted upwards, and she felt her own breath warming his mouth. She wanted him to crush against her, to call from her all that choked, wasted passion which had been hoarding itself, piecemeal, only for him. But the subtlety of his touch held. Now, as she opened to him, he refused to plunder what she so readily offered. Tenderly he drew back, holding her head firm against his chest.

'Don't do that, Rosie,' he said gently. 'Don't offer yourself like that . . .'

She blinked uncertainly. 'Was I offering myself?' she asked weakly, looking down at the forest-green skirt, neat across her lap. The colour was dense, impenetrable, the wool crêpe absorbing all light into its sombre depths. She sighed shakily. 'Now I really don't understand,' she added mournfully.

He came to sit beside her on the sofa, and looked
hard into her dark eyes. The lashes were still moist and
spiky from her tears.

'I can wait, Rosie,' he said softly. 'I can wait until
you want me body *and* soul. You'd regret it if we made
love now. Later, soon, you'll want me unreservedly. I
shall wait until then.'

'Will I?' she asked drily, the fragments of her mind
beginning to come together.

'Oh, yes,' he said softly, and when she looked across
the planes of his high cheekbones into his eyes she knew
that he was being absolutely sincere, for once. He really
believed that if he hung on he could make her fall in
love with him all over again.

'You may just have blown your big chance,' she said
wryly, a crooked smile breaking on her lips.

He shook his head. 'No. I don't take advantage of
women in tears. Or in punts. I waited then—I can do it
again. I haven't lost anything. You'll see, when the time
comes.'

'You really have blown it,' she said, almost grinning
now. 'Haven't you realised yet that all these reminders
of times past only serve to harden me? If you'd pre-
tended to be a reformed character, no longer seeing
Emma, I doubt I'd have been able to hold out for an
hour. But whenever I remember that time . . . well . . .'

He blinked, then looked away into the fire. Something
bitter, resigned, had shadowed his features. 'You really
can't forgive, can you?'

'You want the moon and the stars, Jack. You expect
me to forgive without one damned thing having changed.
You haven't apologised. You've never even asked for my
forgiveness,' she responded stiffly.

'No,' he said softly. 'And I won't. I'd like you to
forgive me for being such a . . . well, "rat" is your word,

isn't it? I hurt you very badly, I know that, and I wish it hadn't had to be that way.'

He paused, then added determinedly, 'But I can't regret what I did. I was only trying to protect Emma's feelings in it all. I had no idea that your bitterness ran so deep—that finding out that she was my sister would destroy us so completely.'

Sister? Was that the word he'd used? It must have been a slip of the tongue. Emma was *her* sister. Not his. Or perhaps she'd misheard...

While she sat, trying to figure out what it was he had meant to say, he got to his feet, then walked across to the occasional table by the fire and poured her a cup of tea. He brought it to her, then went back to his seat. He seemed to be waiting for a response to his words, but she was completely at a loss as to what to say.

'I thought you didn't care that I'd had to be hurt,' she muttered at last, a frown puckering her brow.

'Of course I cared,' he replied caustically. 'But I...well, Emma's *my* sister too, Rosie. Surely you've accepted by now that it's only natural that I cared for her and wanted to protect her? I can see that the shock knocked you sideways at the time, but you've had four years to get used to the fact.'

Rosie actually stopped breathing. His sister? When she at last tried to swallow the action made a harsh, cracking noise in the back of her throat.

'Sister...?' she said hoarsely, her mouth quite parched.

He didn't seem to register her shock. He was leaning forwards, his elbows on his knees, his fingers locked.

'When my father and your mother met up again I was a grown man, living my own life. It should have made little difference to me that I had a new stepmother so soon after my own mother had died. And in fact I can't say that I was unduly bothered—until I went out to Italy and met my new sister. Emma was seventeen, and awkward and shy and very confused. I took her under my wing, I suppose. Your mother and my father were wrapped up in each other, and, anyway, your mother felt guilty enough about having left you behind, without Emma loading fresh troubles on to her as well. Emma needed a listening ear, and I took on that role.'

Rosie tried to close her parted lips but they wouldn't move. Her mouth was bone-dry. She looked fuzzily at the cup of tea, but there was no strength in her hands to lift it. His *stepsister*. Emma was his stepsister. That was why he cared for her. Why any child she and Jack might have would be more than a common-or-garden nephew or niece to Emma. She would be an aunt *and* a step-aunt—if there was such a thing as a step-aunt—at one and the same time... Yes, she could see that anyone might think that that was quite an achievement... And *that* was why she lived in New York and he lived in England and yet there was still a bond... Stepbrother and sister. Yes. They hadn't been planning for her to provide the child they wanted... They hadn't been lovers at all... Oh, no... no... Her breathing became shallow and fast; her mind was whirling...

'She was a mess, Rosie,' he said heavily. 'The family she'd loved all her life had just collapsed in ruins around her. She wanted so desperately for her mother to be happy with my father—it was plain that they loved each other, but they certainly had a few teething troubles in that first year or so. I tried to help Emma come to terms with it. I certainly felt protective. Of course, I should never have consented to play the role I did as far as you were concerned, but at the time her needs were very real to me. You were just a cardboard figure—heard of, but never met. Emma wanted me to look you up and try and patch things up between the two of you. She persuaded me that it would be best if I got to know you myself first, without revealing our relationship. I guess

I was so concerned about how it was going to help Emma that I never took time out to consider how it might all come to affect you. I had a few qualms, I must admit, when I drove up to the house. And then suddenly you were there in front of me, terribly real, blushing furiously, your eyes shining, and mud all over your jeans.

'I was entranced by you. Sufficiently entranced to tell you my name straight away. I expected you to know enough about your mother's new husband for the name to mean something... For it all to come tumbling out there and then and the deception to be over before it had begun. But my name obviously meant nothing to you at all. You didn't realise that there was a link with Emma, and within hours I knew that I wanted it to stay that way. I was falling in love with you, and I didn't want anything to come between us.'

'But if only you'd told me...' whispered Rosie, her eyes huge in her ashen face.

'I couldn't. Don't you see? I thought that if I told you too soon—if I didn't give whatever was developing between us time to mature—that you might get angry and stop seeing me. I didn't want to risk it. I was falling in love with you and I couldn't help myself. I thought, you see, Rosie, that once we were married you'd come to understand. That you'd learn to see it from her point of view, and even if you didn't it wouldn't matter...'

He shrugged helplessly. The eyes that were turned to hers were weary. She wanted to reach out and stroke his eyelids with the tip of her finger. But she was afraid to move. Afraid that the spell would break and all his words would shatter into lies again. He always told lies, didn't he? She'd been training herself to remember that. But this wasn't a lie. It wasn't a lie and none of it was and he'd loved her and he wanted her still and it was all— every word of it—the truth... The honest truth.

'I felt that I couldn't betray her,' Jack continued, so intent on explaining that he failed to register the effect all this was having on her. He turned his face towards Rosie. 'So I can't ask for your forgiveness, Rosie. But I damned well wish I had it all the same. I was crazy with love for you. I've made it plain that I still want you. But you've got to be the one to apologise. Because you can be absolutely certain that I won't.'

This time the ringing in her ears was louder than before. The sense of disbelief was stronger, if that were possible. This time there was no plate-glass door close at hand, no summer storm beyond to envelop her, no overwhelming urge to hide her pain. Because this time there was no pain to hide. Only happiness, relieving an ache so ingrained, so deep, that she had long since ceased to acknowledge its presence. This time she really did faint, her limbs crumpling as she hit the floor, the tea weeping into the carpet.

CHAPTER EIGHT

'SHE'S been looking pale all day. She's been under some stress lately, so at first I thought that was the reason...'

'She's young and strong. Much more likely to be a virus. A couple of days' complete rest, in any case. If she's still off-colour then, we can run some tests.'

Rosie opened her eyes just in time to see a portly pin-striped figure exiting from the room. Then her view was blocked by Jack's face swimming close to her own.

'Jack?' she mumbled.

'Shh. You fainted. Nothing to worry about. I put you to bed and asked my next-door neighbour to pop in and take a look. He's very good. He says its a virus.'

'It's not,' she replied, but his finger came down on her lips to silence her.

'You're supposed to rest,' he said solicitously.

She shook her head against the pillow, conscious as she did so that there was no collar rubbing against her neck. A quick pat under the bedclothes established that she was down to her bra and pants. She smiled, remembering.

'You undressed me!'

'No tight clothing... I remembered that from my Boy Scout days. Don't worry,' he added Boy Scoutishly, 'I kept my eyes closed.'

'It's OK,' she murmured.

'You're not well,' he said, frowning at her suspiciously. 'I'm going to go and let you get some sleep. If you want anything just press this button.' And he indicated an intercom at the side of the bed.

'I want you,' she smiled.

But he just frowned again and left.

Once he had gone she found she was still shaking— with happiness. She slipped out of the huge four-poster bed and crossed the room to survey herself in a mammoth mahogany-framed mirror.

She stood there in her white lacy bra and pants, hugging herself, admiring herself, imagining him peeling back the flimsy underclothes and making love to her just as he had done then.

'His stepsister!' she squeaked, rubbing excitedly at her upper arms and shivering with pleasure. She blew an offending tendril of hair away from her face, and then, feeling weak with joy, ran back to the bed and snuggled under the clothes. Should she press the buzzer now and tell him? In a minute. She would just lie here relishing the knowledge for a little. For years she had racked her brains, looking for the answer that would make it all come right. Now she had it.

To her surprise the next time she opened her eyes it was morning. How could she have slept so deeply when she had such important news to tell Jack? Her hand darted out and pressed hard on the buzzer. Jack came in and half opened the curtains. He was wearing a fresh dark suit with a crisp blue and white striped shirt.

'Where did you get those clothes?' she asked, bleary from sleep.

He looked at her oddly. Then came and put a hand on her forehead. She smiled up at him.

'I'm not delirious. I just couldn't work out how you'd got fresh clothes without disturbing me.'

He peered into her eyes. 'I keep clothes at my pent-house at the office. I spent the night there,' he muttered. 'Why? Are you afraid I might have ravished you while you were asleep?'

'Mmm . . . what a nice idea,' she said, and reached her arms up to his neck.

But he straightened his back and took his hand from her forehead. 'How are you feeling?' he asked dubiously.

'Better than I've felt for years.' Rosie sat up, feeling yesterday's smile stretch her cheeks into tight apples. Her hair hung tangled over her shoulders. She watched his eyes as they were drawn to her breasts, lace-clad, peeping through the strands of hair. She beamed at him.

He cleared his throat. 'Do you think you could manage a light breakfast?'

'You bet. I'm starving. And Jack . . . I've got something to tell you . . .'

'I'll get Mrs Reeves to send something up. I'm afraid I have appointments this morning, but I'll get the doctor to——'

'Jack! Listen! What you said yesterday—before I fainted. Jack, I didn't know. Don't you understand?'

He looked at her intently, shaking his head.

'Oh, Jack! I didn't realise that you were Emma's brother. I thought that you two were—well, lovers. I suppose that when I said that I'd found out about your relationship you must have thought I meant just that you were related, whereas what I really meant was . . . And, of course, you didn't even try to deny it or explain it, because you wouldn't have thought there was any need . . . Oh, you *do* see, don't you? I can't think why it never struck me that she'd have a whole new set of relatives via Mum's new marriage, and that she might easily love people whom I'd never heard of—in a family sort of way. Anyway, when I overheard that conversation in the foyer, I naturally thought——'

'Stop. I can already imagine what you naturally thought.' Jack's eyes were wide with disbelief. Slowly he came towards her and sat on the edge of the bed. She

wanted him to reach out and touch her, but he didn't.
He didn't even look especially pleased. Just surprised.

'I know this must seem quite absurd to you. I mean,
if you'd assumed that what I discovered that afternoon
was that you two were sister and brother, then you must
have thought my reasons for becoming so hysterical and
storming off like that were fairly petty. But, of course,
I thought that you didn't love me at all. That you'd just
been using me, you see. I felt terribly betrayed. Don't
you understand?'

She stopped for a moment to take in the confused
mixture of emotions that were crossing his eyes like
clouds against a blue sky.

'I loved you very much, Jack,' she said softly at last.
'And now that I know the truth, I . . . I love you still.'
And for the second time she opened her arms to him.

He looked long and hard at her before moving. He
didn't come into her arms. But he finally swung his long
legs up on to the bed and put his arm around her, settling his cheek against her head.

'Jack . . . ?' she whispered, longing for him to kiss her,
to wipe away the past forever. Oh, this was marvellous.
All the love she had ever felt for him was pouring back
into her, filling her to overflowing. She wanted him so
much . . .

He pressed his mouth into her hair and inhaled deeply.
'So . . .' he said, his voice soft and low. 'You love me?'

'Yes . . .'

He squeezed her shoulder, pulling her closer against
him, but still not kissing her. She couldn't help feeling
disappointed. He had told her so often in the past weeks
that he wanted her. She had thought she need only explain her mistake and they would immediately be as easy
and happy in each other's arms as they had been all those
years before. Then she remembered how shocked she had
been. Shocked enough to faint clean away. He must be

feeling like that. Of course. But fainting wasn't exactly an option for him.

She looked down the bed at his long, trouser-clad legs on top of the covers. Shyly she snuggled against him, pressing her mouth to the front of his shirt and dropping little kisses against the taut cloth. He sat very still. She must give him time. It wouldn't take long.

She would wait for the shock to pass, and then he would crush her against him and bruise her mouth with kisses. He wanted her. He'd admitted that time and again. And he'd been crazy with love for her when they'd married. He'd said so. She'd grown used to believing it was a charade—to being suspicious. Now she could erase every one of those miserable thoughts. He'd married her because he loved her. He had been tender and gentle and funny and kind. Soon she would meet that man all over again.

How she must have hurt him when all he'd been trying to do was to help her sister. He'd been so loyal to poor Emma. The thought brought sharp tears of sentiment to her eyes. He couldn't have known that Emma had brought it all on herself by persuading their mother to go... Actually, it was rather sad, now she came to think of it... Except that she didn't want to think of Emma. Just Jack. Jack. Jack. Jack. She blinked the tears away, listening to the thud of his heart; relishing the shimmer of desire that was brushing across the surface of her skin.

'Oh, Jack. You must have thought I was crazy. But it honestly never occurred to me that there was any other explanation. When I saw you together I was certain that Emma and you were deeply in love, and that our marriage was just a farce. Can you believe that?'

Jack edged himself into a more comfortable position. 'Yes...' he said pensively, swallowing. And then he swung his legs down off the bed, and stood erect, looking down on her. He reached out a hand and drew a finger down

her cheek to her jaw. 'Well,' he said drily, 'so I have
what I wanted, after all.'

Rosie searched his eyes. 'What's the matter, Jack?
Don't you believe me?' She ran her tongue over her lips
nervously. It was impossible. But he seemed so
distant...so withdrawn all of a sudden. Fear took hold
of her heart and grappled it while she waited for his
response.

'Oh, I believe you,' he said with a gentle grimace. 'It's
just that this changes things. I'd been thinking of you
as... Well, let's just say that I'm very pleased that this
particular earthquake has come along. I want you very
much, Rosie. And now you're mine.'

'Yes,' she said, frightened. Why wasn't he kissing her?
Holding her? What was going wrong?

'Mrs Hellec,' he said with a cynical smile, and reached
out and took her hand.

His felt dry and lifeless in her own. She had to force
her fingers not to dig pleadingly into his.

'I'll get Mrs Reeves to bring you a slap-up breakfast.
I'm afraid I can't wriggle out of these appointments, but
I'll be back about mid-afternoon. We can do whatever
you want then.'

'I know what I want to do...' said Rosie, wanting,
actually, to cry.

He smiled wryly, and then left.

When he came back it was four o'clock. The autumn
sky was heavy and grey. A fine drizzle hung in the dirty
London air.

She had found her suitcase by then, standing neatly
in another of the house's enormous bedrooms. It was a
pretty bedroom, white lace everywhere, with cream and
blue Chinese rugs. Much more feminine than the heavy,
carved four-poster with indigo and ochre drapes, and
the dense Turkish carpet of his bedroom. But it was a
guest room. Not his room. She felt painfully usurped.

She was wearing a light cream wool dress with a sweetheart neckline. She was glad she'd packed it. The light colour was suggestively bridal, which was exactly what she was hoping to be made to feel. She had left her hair loose. He would have got over the shock by now. Surely.

He smiled when he came into the room, and took her hands. There was something almost staid about the gesture. She winced, turning her face away so that he wouldn't read the dismay in her eyes. For seven hours she'd been telling herself that it would be different when he got back. Now she felt ominously uncertain again.

'Have you thought about what you want to do?' he asked. 'Restaurants? Theatres ... ?'

'I had done,' she sighed, 'but somehow I don't think I'm going to get my own way.'

His eyes narrowed. 'What did you have in mind?' he asked, and his voice held none of that old, remembered tenderness.

'I was hoping that you'd make love to me,' she blurted, suddenly angry. 'What did you think? It's been a long time, Jack. I thought you wanted me.'

He dropped her hands. He shoved his own into his pockets and crossed the drawing-room to a drinks trolley. He sloshed a little brandy into a glass, and downed it quickly.

Then he swung around and faced her. 'OK,' he said coolly. He came and took her hand and led her into the guest room where her suitcase had been left. He put his hands on her shoulders and lowered his mouth to hers. He smelt of brandy.

Rosie pulled back from the embrace. 'I've changed my mind,' she muttered furiously.

He just looked at her, a sardonic tilt to his mouth.

'Go on. Say something,' she challenged, her mouth puckered with hurt.

'You're the one who's changed her mind. *You* say something,' he countered coldly.

'All right. I don't want a man who has to take a drink before he can bring himself to make love to me. Nor one who doesn't take me to his own bed. Last time we made love we were husband and wife. Together. Now . . . well, frankly, I feel as if you're merely doing me a favour. When I woke up this morning I thought it was going to be the happiest day of my life. It's gone badly downhill. It certainly won't be improved by being taken to bed by a man who, quite obviously, would rather be at the theatre.'

Jack shrugged. He took off his jacket and flung it on the bed. Then he prised the heavy links from his cuffs and rolled back his shirt-sleeves. He stood facing her, his hands in his trouser pockets, his forearms corded and tense beneath the mantle of sleek dark hairs. There was something soberingly grey behind the blue brilliance of his eyes.

'OK,' he said. 'Then we won't make love. I've been telling you for some time now that I can wait.'

'You've changed since I told you,' accused Rosie, fighting another rush of tears.

'No,' he said gravely. 'It's you who've changed. Finding out that Emma is my sister has changed your view of me. But don't forget that I always assumed that you knew. Nothing has changed for me, except you.'

Rosie swallowed. 'But I've changed from hating you to loving you. Is that bad?'

'No. Of course not. But it's fairly dramatic.'

'Then . . . I don't understand.'

'When I wanted you, Rosie, yesterday and all those days before, I wanted someone who didn't love me.'

'It's funny, Jack, I never had you down as a spoiled brat.'

'Is that how you see it? Someone who doesn't want something just because it's an offer?'

'What else am I supposed to think?'

'Why don't you try asking yourself why I wanted to make love with you so much when I knew damn well you didn't love me?'

Rosie hesitated. He didn't love her any more. It would have been OK—square somehow—if they neither of them had loved the other. If they were simply re-creating a passion which had once been based on love, but which was now based on something...different. She was right. She knew it.

'I see,' she said heavily. 'My loving you isn't quite enough, is it?'

He didn't speak. But his dark head inclined forwards a little, in a grave nod.

'I'll go,' she said bravely, thinking that when she did she would die of grief. 'I can get a train back to Dorchester and a cab from there. I quite understand, Jack. It's been a long time. I must have been a little crazy today not to have realised that.'

'No.' His voice was level but determined. 'You're not going, Rosie. You're my wife. You're going to live with me and we're going to make things come right. I won't let you go now. Not for any reason.'

'I don't mean this unkindly, Jack. But I honestly don't think I want to be the wife of a man who—who has reservations. I want to be loved for what I am. I'm not pleading or anything. If it's not right for you, then I'll have to accept it. But let's not prolong the agony, huh? At least this way we've got some very good, very old memories. Let's leave it that way.'

'Rosie?' The word was a question. His hand came out and lay like swansdown on her shoulder.

She hoped he couldn't feel her trembling. 'It's better, Jack. You must know that. And this time I have the

consolation of knowing that all those memories are worth
something after all. That you did love me then. It was
corrosive, believing otherwise. This time it may even
prove constructive.'

The fingers clenched abruptly against her shoulder,
biting down hard.

'But if you stay with me it will be even more constructive. You'll see.'

'I don't think so, Jack...'

'Yes. Your emotions have been frozen for a long
time—as have mine. We must give the thaw time...'

She made the mistake of looking into his eyes. They
were piercingly intense, a clear, straightforward blue. So
he was hoping, as much as she was, that the old feeling
would return for him too?

'I...it would be better if I went...' But she wasn't
sure any more. Her voice wavered slightly.

And then the other hand came and grasped the other
shoulder equally furiously. And the mouth that came
down on hers, growling a heated 'no' against her lips
tasted not of brandy but of him. Something in what she
had said had injected fire into his veins. But what?

It was beyond any of her powers to ignore the land-
slide of molten desire which thundered from nowhere to
consume her. He needed her. His lips told her that. How
could she ever leave now?

She had been waiting for twenty-four hours for him
to kiss her that way. As his mouth moved over hers, hot
and demanding, it wasn't a remembered passion which
roared into life, but a fresh, new-born response to the
man she loved. His firm lips opened over hers. His
tongue probed insistently at hers, parting them, roving
over her teeth until they too opened to him so that their
mouths became one. She found her mouth welcoming
the ruthless conquest of his tongue, found her own

tongue pushing urgently against his own, so that between them roared a battleground of fiery passion.

He pushed her back on to the bed, still kissing her, tumbling beside her, rolling against her so that his thigh parted hers, pressing uncompromisingly between her legs. His flat palm found her breast and closed over it, cradling the full swell of its roundness in his hands, before seeking out the excited nipple with the heel of his hand and grinding it with a slow, circular motion. She was unable to cry aloud, but a shudder ran the length of her spine in reply to the spearing pleasure the rhythmic pressure drew forth.

Her arousal gathered pace to match the dominance of his own need. He was exciting her by the swift insistence of his mouth and hands, by the hard force of his male body, which leaned demandingly into her own at every curve and hollow. There was a desperation about the way he was taking her. The compelling importance of his desire answered the cry of her own once imprisoned passion, now bursting free to course madly through her veins. She felt the heat of it pulse upwards, throb outwards, till her skin was flushed with it, her breasts prickled with it, her nipples bloomed hard with it. Until she was thrusting against the solid hardness of his muscular thigh, arching her soft flesh against the powerful sweep of his chest, begging him to bid more of her.

When he came to undress her he kept one knotted hand against her head, raking rhythmically through the long strands of her hair, holding her desire captive during the unendurably long minutes it took him to draw her flesh free of her garments. He stripped himself bare in seconds, coming before her like a raging god, packed muscle taut beneath golden skin, shining with sweat. The pattern of hair on his chest, his belly, his flanks, coarse and dark against the sheen of his skin, made her cry a wild 'yes!' into the still air of the room. She had forgotten how he looked naked until now, but the recognition was so instantaneous, so potent that it alone nearly tipped her desire into ecstasy.

He knelt, straddling her legs, hovering over her, tendons stretching his skin into taut columns. Then his mouth came down first on one breast and then the other, plucking at her roused nipples, taunting them with his tongue, forcing sweat to break on her skin as she arched against him feverishly, sobbing out her need. Her head lifted forward so that her own lips could reach for his hair-roughened chest, nibbling and tugging and pulling with a wanton mindlessness, while his mouth freed her breasts to the possession of his broad palms.

At last, in a kind of anguished unison, they slid their hands to each other's shoulder-blades, and he lowered himself down upon her. His shoulder was on her cheek. She could taste him. His fingers dug hard into her back. She was rising to meet him, climbing towards him, until the hard curve of his buttocks clenched with the first thrust.

As soon as he was inside her she curled around him like an animal, her legs clutching him, her heels urging him, her arms encircling him, while he ground into her, hard, desperate, gripped by the utter compulsion of his carnal need. As he spilled his passion, roaring his ecstasy against her tangled hair, her own body convulsed into a spasm of pleasure, the inner pulses hammering while the outer world blackened against her closed eyes. The sense of release was overwhelming. For a long age she seemed to fall through a blood-red darkness, until at last the frenzy resolved into faint ticking, like the death-throes of a discarded watch.

Her voice moaned out each exhausted breath. His skin eased slightly against her own, and then he became still, a spent weight, drained, replete, burningly warm.

At last they fell apart, side by side, eyes closed, breathing ragged. It was as if both sensed a completeness in the other, wrought by the violence of their union, which was too fragile to disturb. There were no tender kisses. No sweet murmurings. No grave fingers tracing the contours of bruised lips. Only the silence of an animal satisfaction, achieved at last.

When the sweat had dried on their skin, when their breathing became even, Rosie sensed his head turning towards her own. Her eyes opened to his, dark and large. His eyes were almost closed still, a dull mist of indigo behind the fringe of short, dense lashes. He surveyed her thus, over the angular planes of his high cheekbones, as if reluctant to open his eyes wide to encompass her. She looked away, her mouth uncertain.

'It was good,' he said, his voice low and rough.

'Yes,' she agreed weakly, her face still turned away. And then she sat up, her back to him, and hugged her knees. She didn't want him to look at her body. Or, at least, not until he could look at it with love. A kind of instinctive shame, a prescience of original sin, swept over her, and coloured her skin. She steeled herself to get to her feet and take a white towelling robe from a hook on the back of the door. She kept her back to him while she donned it, and then returned to the bed.

He didn't comment on her display of modesty, and when she dared look at him his eyes were fixed hard upon the ceiling, as if he acknowledged, too, the rightness of her propriety.

'I still think I'd better go,' she sighed, running her fingers through her hair.

He looked at her then. A steely, uncompromising look. 'No,' he said. 'You'll stay. I married you because I loved you. We'll stay together. Things will change. I will. You will.'

'I won't change. I don't think I can.' She gave him a look of such bleak sincerity that she doubted the wisdom of opening herself to him so entirely. But she kept her eyes fast upon his, despite the inner promptings to look away. She didn't want to make him feel sorry for her, nor guilty at his own lack of proper emotion. But she knew that only if she were honest with him would she ever be able to live with herself in the years to come.

He folded his hands behind his head, and looked once more at the ceiling. She followed the line of his high brow, studying the short dark hair, streaked with grey. She wanted to stroke his forehead tenderly and soothe him and tell him that it would be all right—even though she didn't believe that it would. Because she loved him and wanted more than anything in the world to make him happy.

And then, unexpectedly, he turned to her again and met her eyes. 'You will change, Rosie,' he said forcefully. 'I'll damned well make you.'

She cupped her hands over her face, rubbing anxiously at the bridge of her nose with one index finger. She looked down at her hands, at the rough white towelling cloaking her knees, and felt suddenly afraid. She loved him so desperately. But she didn't know him at all. She knew only that he was a man who would have his way.

CHAPTER NINE

JACK insisted that they stay in London for a while. He was attentive and charming when he was with her. At times she felt like a dinner-party guest. She certainly didn't feel like the mistress of the Harley Street house, though Mrs Reeves and the rest of the small staff all treated her very much as if she was. She felt like an impostor as she decided on dinner menus and ordered waxy, florist's flowers for Mrs Reeves to arrange, down in the bowels of the house.

Jack worked hard. He took her to the stark, modern office block which housed the British arm of Hellec Quebec Estates Ltd and introduced her to his secretary, who was a reassuringly frowsty female, and his PA, who was devastatingly glamorous, and reassuringly male. Also to a variety of heads of department who proved a random mixture of frosty and glamorous, female and male. One or two, who were both glamorous and female, frightened Rosie a little, and might have frightened her more, except that she couldn't for the life of her see why she should fear them when Jack was so very determined to make her truly his wife, regardless of the fact that he didn't love her. He had proved time and again that he desired her—always with that compelling urgency which had characterised their first reunion. And always, since then, in the darkness of night. But jealousy had a habit of niggling at her none the less, now that she loved him all over again.

The first day he had arranged for the next-door doctor to come and see her again. She had been foolishly pleased. There was obviously no virus—and yet he was taking such pains to look after her. In fact the doctor had scarcely bothered to enquire about her health. He had come to advise her on contraception. Afterwards she had stared hard at the little foil pack of pills and had to restrain herself from throwing them on the fire. She'd consoled herself that it would be an empty gesture. If she did, she'd only have to find another doctor and get herself some more. If Jack didn't want to father a child on her, then she didn't want to bear him one. It was only Emma who had ever wanted him to become a father, anyway.

The second day he had taken her shopping, and had provided her with a long strip of credit cards so that she could fill in the time while he worked with more shopping.

'Why on earth should I want to keep shopping?' she asked. 'Haven't we bought enough?'

He shrugged. 'I'm very busy at work just at present. It would be something for you to do.'

Rosie, who had never been bored in her life, surveyed him with dismay. Just who, exactly, did this long-lost husband of hers think she was? She almost took off back to Dorset at that point.

But then he said, 'You do like nice clothes—and you don't mind spending to get them. I thought it might be a treat for you to indulge yourself while I'm so tied up.'

It wasn't exactly an answer to set her pulses racing, but at least it was fair comment. Not reason enough to abandon him, anyway. She was very conscious that he'd spent four years believing that she'd abandoned him once for the flimsiest of reasons. No doubt that was why he still had his doubts...

On the third day she pocketed her credit cards and went out and ordered a drawing-board, and a huge range of pigments and coloured inks, brushes and pens. He

took her out to dinner that evening, and introduced her
to a party of friends as his wife, tucking his arm possessively around her waist, his voice like tar trickling over
loose gravel. He didn't mention to any of them that she
was an interior designer. Just that she was his wife. She
saw envy in the women's eyes, and wished that they could
see her at work in her studio, and envy her that. At least
her work was real—whereas this charming husband of
hers, who treated her so possessively in public, and so
politely in private, was a sham.

Anyway, the actress in her managed to arrange a
suitably simpering smile on her features and kept the
small talk flowing for her for the duration of the meal.
She had agreed to stay with him. To try to re-establish
their marriage. It would have been very wrong to have
given the outside world any hint of the less than perfect
nature of their liaison.

On the seventh day the drawing-board arrived.

'What the hell is that?' asked Jack, as Rosie directed
the delivery men to one of the more modest guest rooms.

'Isn't it obvious?'

'So you want to keep on working? Why? I've made
quite a lot of progress with this factory business. I've
engaged a really clever guy to run the outfit. Top art
school background, and admin experience, too. He's got
plenty of your designs to be getting on with. You don't
need to do anything.'

'Don't I?' she flared, her anger stirred to a billowing
froth. 'So you think any old person with the right sort
of background can do my job, huh? How dare you? This
is my business. It's based on my talent. You have no
right to use my designs. Where did you get them from
anyway?'

'You left them at Aubrey's,' he said coolly. 'And in
case you're interested I've been delegating a great deal
of my own work in recent days, too. I'm taking you

abroad for a couple of months. An island in the Indian ocean. A kind of belated honeymoon.'

She was too cold with anger to burst into tears. 'We've had our honeymoon, Jack,' she said nastily. 'I can't think of anything worse than being marooned with you on a desert island. Conversation would be pointless. You only ever ask me what I've bought. We'd be reduced to silence within minutes. And we can hardly make love all day!'

'We did once,' he said in low, dangerous tones.

'Not the way we make love now,' she countered brusquely. And then she turned her back and went to supervise the setting up of her workroom. He didn't refer to the holiday again. It was the first time she had got her own way.

Marguerite came up to town for some discussions on Littlebourne Hall. She had agreed to supervise things in Rosie's absence. They met up with Aubrey for a leisurely business lunch. Jack took Rosie along without bothering to tell her who the company would be. Aubrey flattered Marguerite and Rosie. Marguerite flattered Jack and Aubrey. Jack flattered Rosie and Marguerite. Rosie sat as still as possible, her mouth smiling but her eyes betraying her.

Over coffee Marguerite said, 'Jack, I must have some time alone with Rosie. We've got a lot of outstanding work back in Dorset to discuss.'

Jack inclined his head, and Rosie smiled very agreeably, though her mouth was dry with fear. What on earth would she tell Marguerite once they were alone?

She needn't have troubled her mind. Marguerite set the agenda quite firmly from the outset.

'What's going on, Rosie?'

'Didn't Dad tell you . . . ? I rang him a couple of days after I arrived in London. Jack and I are married.'

'Yes. He told me that. I think he'd guessed, anyway.'

'He's very wise...' pondered Rosie, wondering how much else her father might have guessed.

'Not that wise. Not wise enough to realise that those sweaters of his do him no favours at all.' She gave Rosie a generous smile. 'So when did you marry him, you dark horse?'

'Actually, we married in haste when we first met, four years ago.'

'And now you're repenting at leisure?'

'No... not that. It's just—well, we've years of mis-understandings to plough through. It can be a bit sticky at times.'

'Do you love him?'

Rosie nodded. 'Yes. I wouldn't be here if I didn't.'

Marguerite pursed her cinnamon lips. 'That's all right, then. After all, he loves you too. It'll be OK.'

'Pardon?'

'You know. Those nine words he said when I first met him.' Marguerite splayed her fingers and ticked off the words one by one. ' "I love her. And I'm going to have her..." Nine... That must be it. Or nine other words to the same effect, anyway. The first three are definitely right.'

Rosie felt her face flush a bright red. He'd said that. He'd said it just days after meeting her again. He couldn't have meant it, though. Or, if he had, then he'd changed his mind fairly sharply, once he got to know her a bit better. Whichever way you looked at it, it wasn't a comfortable thought.

One night Jack stayed at his suite of rooms on top of the glass box. He rang Rosie to let her know.

'Will you be all right? Mrs Reeves can see to everything.'

'Of course I'll be all right. It's not as if we... It will be nice to have some time to catch up on my reading.'

'We what?'

'Pardon . . . ?'

'You started to say that it's not as if we something-
or-other. What were you going to say?'

'Nothing.'

'Rosie!' He sounded quite peremptory. 'Tell me.'

She could almost see his straight brows gathering into
a frown. 'Honestly. It doesn't matter.'

'If we'd talked more before, then we might not have
ended up in this mess. So start talking.'

The unfairness of it! Rosie's temper snapped. 'Good
grief! You were the one who didn't tell me that you were
Emma's brother. You may have thought I'd realised when
I saw the two of you together, but when you came to
the house, pretending to be lost, you *knew* I didn't know!
And you quite intentionally didn't tell me. So don't tell
me *anything* about getting things out in the open, Jack
Hellec!'

'I take your point. But even so, you're the one who
keeps the taboos intact. You're the one who won't talk
now.'

Rosie took the receiver away from her ear to make
appalled faces at it. 'I'm damn well not! And, if you
must know, what I was going to say before I stopped
myself was that it wasn't as if we had a lot to talk about.
Meaning that you come home in the evening and talk
about the weather and current affairs. I can get that from
the television, thank you. So there!'

And then she slammed the phone down. She didn't
know whether or not she hoped it would bring him haring
back to Harley Street. But it didn't. And she didn't care.
She spent the evening at her drawing-board and sat up
very late designing a set of bathroom tiles. Pastel-
coloured sweet peas on white; a repeating border.
Working was a good antidote to Jack. It was as calming
as he was disturbing.

She didn't miss him at all until she climbed into the
big four-poster. There was far too much room in it for
one. She threshed about, trying to relish all the space.
It didn't work. Her body was aching for him. Time and
again she had asked herself, as the days turned into
weeks, why she was staying on. The spurious charm
which he lavished on her went no way to concealing the
fact that he still didn't love her. The way he turned away
from her when she let herself begin to chatter naturally
underlined the fact that he didn't even like the real Rosie.
The relaxed, voluble Rosie. He wanted the attractive
pretence, preferably dressed in well-cut, expensive
clothes, bought, symbolically, with his money.

She rolled to the centre of the bed, where usually his
big, hard body could be found. The empty space tugged
at her heart-strings. Because whenever she asked herself
why she was staying she could only find one answer. She
needed his lovemaking. She needed him to turn to her
in the dark, with that charged desperation which lay
behind every kiss. She needed him to arouse her with
his own need. To want her. And this night he wasn't
there, and suddenly there was no reason for staying any
more.

Absurdly, she remembered her jeans and her trainers—
presumably still puddled on her bedroom floor—back
at her father's house. She felt comfortable in her jeans
and trainers. And she hadn't done any gardening for
such a long time. She remembered the handle of her own
trowel, smooth wood, fitting her hand. She began to
sob. Great racking sobs which carried on well into the
night, and which left her pale and drawn in the morning.

He came back for a lateish breakfast, and found her
wallowing in the bath. He looked briefly at her, and then
turned his back, taking off his jacket, and peeling his
shirt off over his head without bothering to undo all
the buttons.

She ran her tongue over her lips. 'What are you doing?'

'Getting changed.'

'Oh.'

'Why? Did you hope I'd come and join you in the bath?'

'Er—I'm just getting out, actually. My fingers have gone pruney.'

She had glimpsed him in daylight, of course, since that first time when they'd made love in the guest room in the late afternoon. Getting out of bed at six every morning. In and out of the bathroom and dressing-room. But mostly he would cover himself circumspectly in a towelling robe. And it was only glimpses, anyway, as he moved to and fro. Now, with his back to her, she could see once again the familiar pattern of muscle stretched over bone. She could see the few coarse, dark hairs which peppered his shoulders and the small of his back. *His back*. Motionless before her. She dipped her eyes to discover that her nipples had hardened at the sight. She reached up a hand and let down her knot of hair so that it curtained her breasts. The ascending wave of desire was, fortunately, much less visible.

He turned to look at her, unfastening his trousers. 'Would you like me to come and scrub your back?' he asked drily, his voice dark as pitch.

Taken aback by the turn of events, she looked at him blankly.

He wandered over to the side of the bath and sat on the edge. He dipped the tips of his fingers in the water and trailed them around the edge of her face, leaving marks like tearstains on her skin. Then his fingers twined into her hair, preparing to lift it away from her breasts; to look at her; to touch her; maybe to make love to her, here in the bath. In daylight.

She shook her head decisively, so that he drew his hand back sharply. She was almost panic-stricken at the thought. She could cope with the pattern they had established, nightly, in the dark. Then, drained, she could fall into a dreamless sleep, preparing herself for the daytime charade. She could keep going like that for a little while longer, at least. But anything more and she would be lost.

'Why did you let your hair down?' he asked, his voice still thick and deep.

'It sort of fell down,' she said weakly. 'Now if you don't mind . . .'

He strode out of the room. 'I know. If I don't mind, your fingers are going all pruney,' he muttered tersely as he went.

When she had scrambled into her robe she went into the bedroom to find him dressed in cords and a lilac-grey lambswool sweater.

'Aren't you going back into work?' she asked, finding her hairbrush and tugging it through the damp ends.

'No.'

'Any reason?'

'I thought we could have breakfast together. And talk. And then perhaps we could drive down to Dorset.'

'Oh!'

Her eyes must have lit up like beacons at the mention of Dorset, because he turned a sardonic smile on her and said, 'I'm pleased that at least part of my suggestion meets with your approval.'

She was too delighted to pay any attention to the taunt. 'It will be lovely to be back in the country again,' she burst out. 'In fact, I was just wondering this morning whether I might pop back for the day to fetch my jeans and trainers.'

'But you could buy some here.'

'Oh, Jack! Haven't you ever worn jeans? New ones are horrible. They're like cardboard, and the buttonhole is so stiff that when you want to go to the loo you practically—— Well. I'm sure you can imagine. But anyway, new jeans are awful, and if you buy the stone-washed ones to get them ready broken-in then they don't last any time at all and go into holes at the knees. So you do have to get new ones now and then, but you alternate them with the old ones until they're old too. Of course I suppose I could have bought a pair and asked Mrs Reeves to put them through the wash about thirty times but——'

He cut across her. '*But* if you don't hurry up and get dressed our breakfast will be cold.'

'You,' she accused, disappearing into the dressing-room to find a comfortable corduroy skirt and a silk blouse, 'are supposed to be the one who wants me to talk. And yet when I do you shut me up.'

He didn't reply immediately, but when she emerged fully dressed he looked up from his Rolex and said, 'Five minutes. Again. You're very consistent.'

'And so,' she muttered caustically, 'are you.'

Their attempts at real talk during breakfast were excruciating. It wasn't helped by the fact that Jack kept breaking bits off his bare toast and buttering them. It reminded her, of course. As if she needed any extra reminding this morning—of all mornings—after he'd come into the bathroom and been so tantalisingly different.

At last Rosie burst out, 'I don't understand what we're supposed to be talking about. If you wish to announce that you've fallen deeply in love with me at last, why don't you just get on with it? I won't complain that it isn't the most romantic of settings. I promise.'

Jack sighed, setting down his knife heavily. 'That isn't what I had in mind,' he said wearily.

Disappointment settled like lead in her stomach. 'I didn't really think it was,' she sighed.

He kept on looking at her, his eyes dark blue and intense.

'It's no good looking at me like that,' she said mournfully at last. 'I feel like a contestant on a quiz show who can't get the answer to the easiest question of all. I don't know what you want me to say.'

He still went on staring silently at her.

'Do you want me to pack my bags?' she asked finally. 'Is that why you're taking me back to Dorset? So I can move back home?'

'This is your home,' he said harshly. 'This and Littlebourne Hall. You'll do well to remember it.'

Her chin rose defiantly. 'Only for as long as I choose, Jack. I'm my own master.'

'So you've taken great pains to prove. Turning our home into a studio, when there's no need! Refusing almost perversely to spend any more of my money than you have to. And the meals! They have to be the worst sort of joke! Can't you even try to be a wife to me, Rosie, for as long as it takes?'

'What's wrong with the meals?' she challenged, too outraged by that particular accusation to pay much attention to the end of his diatribe.

'Brown Windsor soup! That's what's wrong with the meals. Steamed plaice with a lemon wedge. Jam tart. You *have* to be doing it intentionally.'

Rosie threw up her hands. 'I thought those were the sorts of meals I was supposed to be ordering! I haven't any experience of sending down instructions to the kitchens.'

'But your father has a housekeeper.'

'Yes. But she's my friend. I just ask her to get the sort of things Dad and I like. Liked. It's different. I don't know what to do here.'

'Well, why don't you do the same thing here? Or do you *like* brown Windsor soup?'

'Not much. But it's the sort of thing you see on menus. It seemed appropriate.'

He sniffed. 'Mrs Reeves tells me she had to dig out an old wartime recipe book to find out how to make it.'

Rosie glared at him. And then she began to laugh. 'Oh, dear. Still, I expect we must be getting terribly healthy. Weren't wartime rations supposed to be good for you...?' And her shoulders started to shake.

Jack didn't laugh, though. He crashed his fist down on the table, setting the cups rattling. 'Dammit, Rosie! Don't you see that that's the point? If you found it a problem, why didn't you discuss it with me? Instead of which you just dredged up some buried memory of a tatty, plastic-covered, set-price menu and spewed out the contents on a daily basis. You can hardly claim to have given the matter any thought at all. Whereas your work... Well...you never seem to think of anything else!'

Rosie had managed to suck hard enough on her cheeks to quell her mirth while he was ranting, but the minute he fell silent she began shaking with laughter again. She hadn't laughed properly for weeks. Now it all spilled out, uncontrollably.

He shoved back his chair, and with a look of utter disgust he left the room. She rested an elbow on the table and covered her eyes, still laughing. Until she started to cry.

Jack had a CD player in his car with quadraphonic sound. They were both glad of it on the long drive down. Littlebourne Hall looked wonderful, bathed in the mellow light of afternoon, especially to the accompaniment of Beethoven's Fifth. The Virginia creeper, which mingled with the evergreen ivy over one side of the house, was a breathtaking, flaming red.

Rosie let out a heavy sigh. All this was so tantalising. The man she loved. A home she was certain to love. Her father and her best friend close at hand. It could add up to perfection, if only...

But if only what? She knew that in her heart of hearts she was waiting for Jack to fall back in love with her—which quite clearly wasn't going to happen. And he was waiting for her to fall out of love with him. Which, also, Rosie acknowledged wryly, wasn't going to happen. After all, he didn't like her. He held back from her, was at best restrained and courteous with her. And yet still she loved him. She glanced across at his profile as he parked the car. The thick, short dark hair, brushed back from his high forehead, the straight nose and jutting chin and well-made mouth. And the eyes. Oh, the eyes. They still hurt her more than anything. No. She wasn't going to fall out of love with him. And nor was she going to turn into a well-dressed wife of convenience, ordering sumptuous and inventive meals, arranging her own florist's blooms in her newly purchased vases, so that Jack could have his cake and eat it.

But for as long as she remained Rosie Wells, just as she was, the very person he had once claimed to love, she was a lost cause. That was the Rosie he didn't seem to want at any price.

Marguerite had been busy with the innards of the house, making sure that Rosie's drawings and colour swatches were turned into a handsome reality. The sitting-room, with its French doors looking out on the lichen-speckled loggia, had been transformed from its former gloomy splendour into a light, restful room, where primrose and pale blues jumbled together comfortably. A chintz suite, low, light oak tables, table-lamps so big that they stood on the floor, had taken the

place of the dark red cabbage roses and dusty chand-
eliers. Only the log fire, crackling merrily, was the same.

'Drink?' asked Jack urbanely.

'Yes,' Rosie replied sweetly.

'What will you have?'

The devil niggled at her. This was yet another parody
of a conversation. 'Cocoa. Made with sweetened con-
densed milk, and just a dash of gin,' she simpered.

Jack closed his eyes briefly and poured her a glass of
pale, dry sherry.

'I don't want sherry,' she glowered.

He buzzed one of the ubiquitous intercoms and ordered her cocoa. Then he sat down opposite her and
folded his arms.

'You've been spoiling for a fight all day,' he said
grimly. 'So get on with it...'

Rosie let out another heavy sigh. He was right. She
badly wanted to argue with him, to get all this festering
nonsense out in the open. But she was afraid of losing
him—even what little she had of him. She hated this
arrangement, but she couldn't bear the idea of the
alternative either. She wanted to sleep with him this night
and every night until he forced her to go. It could only
mean, she decided heavily, that she didn't have any pride
left at all.

'Nothing, Jack...' she said wearily.

'That's not true.'

'No, it's not. But it's better than fighting. It would be
pointless.'

'Are you sure? Are you so determined not to change
that you won't risk exposing yourself in a showdown?'

'Jack,' she said pleadingly, 'don't you understand that
I can't change? Any more, it seems, than you can.'

He threw his hands wide, palms open, in a gesture of
angry despair. 'So we just go on like this, until we hate
each other so much that there's nothing to salvage?'

'I won't end up hating you, Jack. I thought I did once. But that was before I knew the truth.'

'So you're quite happy with things the way they are?'

'No. Of course not. But this is the way I'm going to go on playing it. If it ends up with you hating me and us parting, then I guess I'll have to live with it.'

'And yet you claim to love me...' he said with a scathing anger edging his voice.

'I'm sorry that it annoys you so much, but yes, I do. I wish I'd managed to hold on to a bit of self-control when I found out about you and Emma. Then I wouldn't have told you that I'd fallen back in love with you. I'd feel much more comfortable living as your wife if I thought you didn't know. But I was fool enough to mention the fact, and I'm damned if I'm going to start lying now. You can take me as I am or not at all.'

'And loving me doesn't make you want to please me?'

Rosie rubbed at the side of her nose with her middle finger. 'I'd like nothing better. But I'm not going to pretend to be something I'm not. What would be the point? Would you care for me any more if I did pretend? Would that really satisfy you, Jack?'

Her repulsively sweet cocoa arrived at that point. She took one sip and then put it down, picking up the sherry instead.

'So you changed your mind about the cocoa?' he commented drily. He looked thoughtfully into the fire and then asked, 'What would you say if I told you that I want to ask Emma here for Christmas?'

Rosie closed her eyes. So he couldn't bear the idea of spending Christmas alone with her? It was hardly surprising, and yet she was still disappointed. Would it make things easier if Emma were here? Since discovering the truth her bitter feelings towards her sister had almost resolved themselves. There was still the fact that she had talked their mother into leaving, but even that didn't

hurt as it once had. Still, it hurt a little. If the sisters
quarrelled Jack might take Emma's part and Rosie would
find that unbearable. In fact, he probably *would* take
Emma's side. After all, he loved his little sister... Which
was not how he felt towards his wife...

'Er—I'm not sure it would be a good idea...'

Jack leaned forward in his chair and picked up a log.
He threw it hard on the fire, sending a shower of sparks
up the chimney. Then, without looking at her, he got
up and departed for his study, muttering something about
work.

There was a small Metro at the house for the housekeeper's use. Rosie borrowed it and set off to see her
father. Surprisingly he wasn't in either the house or the
stables. She retrieved her jeans and trainers and a couple
of friendly sweatshirts and went back to Littlebourne.
Having changed, she went out to rake leaves from the
huge expanse of lawn. An hour's hard work in the failing
light brought roses to her cheeks and a respectable pile
of twigs and leaves to a quiet corner of the garden. It
was dark when she raided the kitchen for a box of
matches, and cold when she set the bonfire alight.

The flames were soon leaping raggedly into the night,
warming her and consoling her. She could have stood
there forever watching them. But it wasn't long before
the sound of voices broke into her reverie.

'You're an idiot!' Jack's voice held an unfamiliar note
of humour and warmth.

'You're not holding me tightly enough. That's the
problem. Stop being such a gentleman and grab me
properly!' It was unmistakably Marguerite.

'Is that better?'

'Much. Actually, put your hand there...that's right.
Mmm. That's fine.'

Rosie turned her back on the fire to peer into the
darkness. But her eyes were blinded from staring so hard

into the heart of the flames. They perceived only blackness.

'For goodness' sake, Marguerite!' Jack's voice was warmly reproving now.

'Oh, you're just an old prude.'

He gave a throaty chuckle. 'A prude! What a cheek! Just because I dared suggest that a skin-tight skirt and four-inch heels weren't exactly suitable garb for our little adventure.'

Rosie's heart had started to thud. An acid taste soured her tongue. She couldn't believe her ears—and nor would she. There was bound to be a perfectly innocent explanation. She had only to wait.

The innocent explanation appeared quite abruptly, emerging into the light of the fire from the darkness beyond. Marguerite was enveloped both in an expensive camel cashmere coat and Jack. Her heels were making a good job of aerating the lawn, and Jack was doing his utmost to prevent her from keeling over at each step.

'Hi!' exclaimed Marguerite. 'What a gorgeous fire. Jack and I spotted it and decided to come and watch. Jack's brought some chestnuts.'

From the depths of his trouser pocket Jack produced a handful of the shiny, dark nuts. 'There's a sweet chestnut tree overhanging the driveway,' he explained. 'I picked up a few of these when I saw you starting the fire.'

Rosie nodded. 'Great . . .' she murmured.

It couldn't have been more innocent. So why on earth did she feel so jealous? Surely Marguerite would never dream of trying to entice Jack, knowing what she did of the situation? And, to be fair, Jack was only doing the gentlemanly thing in helping Marguerite across the treacherous terrain in those shoes.

There was nothing to it at all. Nothing except the warm timbre of his voice when he spoke to her. Nothing except the relaxed good humour which emanated from the pair of them. She felt painfully excluded. Perhaps her pride was beginning to reassert itself after all.

'I'm going to buy you a pair of brogues, Marguerite,' teased Jack. 'A really hefty pair with half-inch tread on the soles.'

'Do by all means. I shan't wear them, of course.'

'You will if you want to go on working for me. We often decide on furnishings while the builders are still sloshing around in cement. I'm not taking you out on site for discussions in shoes like that. I shall insist.'

'Not brogues, Jack, and that's final.'

'Galoshes, then. A specially constructed pair of galoshes designed to accommodate your sexy shoes.'

The laugh started as a rumble deep beneath Marguerite's breastbone. It exploded into a cluster of snorts before ripping through the night air, full-throated and rich. 'High-heeled galoshes!' she gasped, somewhere in the middle of it. 'Wonderful! I must tell Calvin Klein!'

Marguerite's laugh was irresistible. Jack didn't even *try* to resist it. Within moments he was laughing with her, while she leaned against him, orange and comfortable in the glow of the fire.

It wasn't pride, after all. It was jealousy. Scoring through her like a ragged blade. Making her screw up her face with the bitter anguish of it. Because if Marguerite could allow herself to laugh like that in front of Jack she must like him very, very much indeed. And, judging by the way he was laughing with her, the feeling was reciprocated.

When Rosie had laughed, just that morning, he had walked away, sick with disgust.

CHAPTER TEN

THE next day Rosie woke late. Jack was still beside her in the bed. His hair smelt smoky from the fire. She longed to reach across the pillow and touch it. But she didn't. She had lain awake half the night, tormenting herself. Not just with the idea of Jack falling in love with Marguerite, though she hoped she could trust Marguerite enough to avoid that kind of complication. But the point was, she told herself bleakly, that had things been different it *might* have happened. Without her, Jack might even now be in love with someone who made him laugh, and who teased him, and who kept him bathed in a warm glow twenty-four hours a day.

Instead of which he had her, whom he wanted and didn't want, and who turned him to ice with the sound of her laughter.

Tentatively she reached across and touched his shoulder. 'Jack...?' she breathed. 'Are you awake?'

He rolled towards her, and his arms came out to find her. Then his eyes opened. He drew back just a split-second before she did.

'Rosie...?' His voice had that early morning burr to it. It sent her senses spinning.

'Jack. Yesterday. We never did talk about the important things.'

'Didn't we? But I thought you told me you weren't ready to change. As far as I'm concerned that was conversation enough.'

'But the thing is, Jack, if I'm not going to change, why on earth do you want to keep our marriage going?'

151

He sat up abruptly in the bed, accidentally flouncing the bedclothes so that they exposed her naked breasts. His eye was caught by the expanse of revealed flesh. For a moment he seemed frozen, and then he threw the sheets over her savagely and said in a voice that was raw with emotion, 'We just need time. You'll see. I don't give up easily, Rosie.'

He got out of bed then and strode across the room to the Victorian bathroom, as yet untouched by the decorator's hand. She watched him, bewildered. He was aroused. But there was such a wrathful sense of purpose in the way he moved that she knew he resented her power to move him so. She heard water thunder into the bath from the ancient plumbing. And when he returned he no longer smelt of woodsmoke.

Later, Rosie realised that she needed to speak to Marguerite about her designs. For the first time in her life she felt a reluctance to pick up the phone and dial the number of her closest friend. It was the incentive she had been looking for to introduce herself to Jay Blackler, who was managing the new factory in Dorchester. She borrowed the Metro and set off to find him.

He was three or four years older than herself, cheerful, with thick auburn hair, and a disarmingly open manner. He was also, as Jack had indicated, talented and able. She spent the whole day with him.

By the end of the day she was genuinely excited by the prospect of collaborating with him, though he insisted that she continue to do all the designing herself. He was adamant that he didn't have half her artistic flair. By the time she got back to Littlebourne she was uncommonly happy.

Dinner with her husband soon cured her of that. He was more taciturn than ever. He didn't even seem to know what the weather had been like, let alone be able to manage a discussion on the economy. He went off to his study shortly after they had eaten, and didn't reappear. When she went to bed she found him already there, and fast asleep. It was the first time it had happened, and it unnerved her.

At breakfast the next day she asked, 'What are your plans?' She was wondering if he planned to leave her.

He shrugged. 'For once I don't have any. No work, anyway. Shall we go down to Weymouth and take the boat out? I can arrange a crew within a couple of hours.'

Rosie nodded, feeling stupidly delighted. 'OK. I thought I'd try and get home some time today and pick up my car and see Dad. But it won't much matter whether I go early or late. I can fit in.'

'There are cars here you can use.'

'I know. But it'll be useful if I have my own. And I'd like to see my father. Why don't you come and meet him, Jack?'

Jack shrugged. 'Maybe. I've got to ring the office first and see if anything's cropped up. I can probably give you a lift, anyway.'

She forbore to point out that just moments before he'd said that he had no work to do. To be honest, she didn't really mind. She rather wanted to see her father on his own and tell him all about everything. Perhaps talking to him would sort things out in her mind. She might even make some sort of decision.

It was arranged that they go sailing in the afternoon. Jack pleaded more business calls, but insisted that she take the Metro over to her father's and leave it to be picked up later. So at eleven o'clock she set off back to the house she still thought of as home. Once again her father was absent. And when she tried to start the Fiesta she found that it had a flat battery after being left standing for weeks on end. So she ran the Metro down to the car park of the Farmer's Arms.

She knew her father was there before she even walked into the bar, because Marguerite's bellowing laughter could be heard right outside the door. And Marguerite only ever went to the Farmer's Arms at her father's invitation. Good. It would be nice to see Marguerite again, away from Jack's aura. She had roasted the chestnuts willingly that evening, glad to have an excuse for opting out of the conversation. But she couldn't keep opting out forever, just because Jack liked Marguerite better than he did her. Later she could get her father on his own and talk to him.

Her father was propping up the bar, one arm resting matily on Marguerite's shoulder. Marguerite was wearing a green leather skirt with matching shoes and a cream angora sweater. She, too, was leaning against the bar.

'Hi!' smiled Rosie, approaching them.

'Rosie!' Her father unhooked his arm from Marguerite's shoulder and came and gave his daughter a brief hug. He didn't say anything, but his eyes let her know that he was more than glad to see her.

'Find us a table, Danny,' ordered Marguerite. 'You may think that it's the height of style to lean against this marvellously quaint bar, but we girls don't. We don't want to find the patina of years rubbing off on our sweaters, do we, Rosie?'

'Speaking of patinated sweaters...' Rosie said with a frown '...what's happened to yours, Dad? I haven't seen you in that sports jacket since the last time we went to the cinema.'

'Your father,' said Marguerite, pursing her mulberry lips and leading them over to a corner table, 'has taken off his revolting sweater. Forever.'

Danny gave his daughter a rueful nod, and muttered, 'It's true, old thing. She's thrown the whole lot in the bin. Says she'll buy me a fluffy lemon Jaeger job to

compensate. But it doesn't sound like much of an ex-
change to me.'

'How on earth did you manage that?' laughed Rosie.

Marguerite's reply was to produce a small piece of
marble from her bag and hand it to Rosie for inspection.
It had been carefully crafted to resemble a ring. And
was rather ugly.

'He gave me that. But I said I'd only accept it on
condition he chucked out every knitted garment in his
possession.' There might have been acid in her voice but
her eyes shone with delight.

'It's a home-made engagement ring,' said Danny,
beaming.

Marguerite sighed theatrically, trying to disguise a
beaming smile of her own. 'Of course, I wouldn't be
caught dead wearing a tombstone like that. But that's
what it is in principle, anyway.'

'Dad!' exclaimed Rosie, her dark eyes round with
amazement.

Her father just grinned happily, and then hooked his
arm carelessly back over Marguerite's shoulder. And then
he began to chuckle. And Marguerite began to snort.
And Rosie, too, with enormous pleasure and relief, began
to laugh. It didn't seem like quite the right moment to
tell them that she'd been considering moving back
home—especially as Marguerite wasn't going to be
wasting any time on a lengthy engagement.

'I'm not giving him time to change his mind,' she said
archly.

A little later Danny turned to his daughter with his
eyes glowing. 'You really are pleased for us, aren't you,
Rosie?'

'Oh, yes, of course I am! Why shouldn't I be?'

Her father pulled a face. 'Oh, you know. Your mother.
I'm afraid she and I married for the wrong reasons all
those years ago. Oh, good enough reasons—like com-

panionship and respect and children. But the wrong reasons all the same.'

'I'm delighted that you've fallen in love at long last. Honestly.'

Her father's face coloured warmly. 'I took my time about it, didn't I? But now that I understand what your mother felt all those years ago I appreciate exactly how much she denied herself when she gave him up. And I know that you must understand too, now that you've got back together with the man you love.' He shook his head ruefully. 'There's only poor Emma still out in the cold,' he added quietly.

Rosie swallowed hard. Not only Emma, she thought bleakly. It can be pretty chilly in my house at times...

But nobody could stay miserable for long in Marguerite's company. 'What shall I do for a wedding-dress, Rosie?' she asked with a hefty sigh. 'Not white, of course. Not that the colour is the real problem. It's the style that's plaguing me. I've never seen a floor-length bridal gown with a pencil-slim skirt, have you? I'll have to have it slashed to the thigh in order to teeter down the aisle. Not quite the thing, eh, my dear?'

Later, after much beer and laughter, Rosie said, 'I never thought I'd live to see the day when Dad threw out his sweaters.'

'Nor,' said Marguerite drily, 'did I. But it's only the first of many changes, isn't it, my darling?'

'I'm so happy for you both,' Rosie said sincerely, wishing that Jack loved her so much that she wanted to give up her work and take up shopping instead, just to please him.

And then Danny gave his bride-to-be a kiss.

Which was just exactly the moment that Jack elected to come into the bar. You had to admit, the man had presence. No sooner had he opened the door than the whole place fell silent. He nodded courteously at the landlord, then swiftly made his way across to their table. Similarly courteous nods were distributed to Danny and Marguerite, who had extricated themselves from the embrace at the sudden silence, but he saved speech itself for Rosie.

'So I've found you at last. Do you realise what the time is?' He caught hold of her arm.

'Oh, the sailing!' she exclaimed, hurrying to her feet.

'That's right. The sailing,' he said curtly.

'I'd forgotten.'

'I'm flattered. Now hurry up.'

'But Jack...this is my father... He and Marguerite——'

Jack turned a pair of cool blue eyes on Danny Wells and said, 'I'm pleased to meet you. But I'm afraid we'll have to get to know one another some other time. Rosie and I are rather pressed at the moment...'

And before Rosie could protest further she was being hustled out of the pub by an arm which, from the outside, must have seemed quite charmingly possessive, snuggled as it was around her shoulder. From Rosie's viewpoint, however, it seemed unnecessarily brutal as it clamped her firmly to his side, forcing her to appear to accompany him voluntarily, when nothing, really, could have been further from the truth.

Out in the car park she tore free. 'Did you need to be quite so rude?'

'Did you?'

'I wasn't being rude. I was about to introduce you to my father.'

'You did introduce me to your father. Don't you remember?' And with that he opened the door of his car for her and stood to one side while she got in.

Then he got behind the wheel and said, 'So you forgot that we were going sailing?'

'Yes. But only because——'

'Only because you had something better to do with your time.'

'Only because,' she said furiously, 'he and Marguerite had just announced their engagement. It was a rather major distraction, as it happened.'

The car had been moving along quite smoothly. But at Rosie's words Jack slammed on the brakes, bringing the car to a screeching halt.

'What did you say?' Jack ground out, his eyes blazing as they turned to meet her own.

'Yes. They're getting married in a few weeks. Why are you so shocked?'

And then, as a dark colour swept over his features, she wished she'd never asked the question.

'Because,' he muttered scornfully, 'I expected better of Marguerite.'

Rosie stared stonily ahead, unable to meet his eyes, quite horrified by his response.

The sailing trip was a washout, of course. Jack busied himself with nautical matters at one end of the boat, while Rosie stared out to sea from the other. They didn't bother with a drink in the quayside pub afterwards. They were both too cold. Jack made love with her that night as if it was the only thing in the world that could warm his blood. And the next day a new car, a coupé, was delivered to the door with Rosie's name on it. Guilt, thought Rosie, stroking the bonnet with deadly resignation.

When Rosie stopped to look dispassionately at her situation, she couldn't for the life of her figure out how she had come to get herself into such an awful mess. With Jack, of all people. Yet again.

What had gone wrong? When he'd first come back into her life she'd sworn that she would never let him hurt her. And yet here she was ploughing deeper and deeper into a sea of pain like a sleepwalker. Why had she agreed to live with him as his wife, when he'd actually confessed that he didn't love her, that he didn't want to love her, and that he didn't even want her to love him? Because his lovemaking seemed to whisper something deeper to her heart, that was why. There was something in the way he took her which kept renewing her belief...her faith...that he might come to love her still. And yet, by daylight, no faith had ever seemed so absurdly misplaced.

He hated her involvement with her work—more and more as time went by. Which, ultimately, spoke volumes about his feelings for her. He loved Marguerite's involvement with her work. He saw Marguerite more and more frequently. Which, ultimately, spoke volumes about his feelings for Marguerite. And every time she mentioned her father's wedding he froze her off. He point-blank refused to meet the man, and claimed that he would have to be abroad for the actual date. He couldn't have made it plainer that the idea of Marguerite's marriage upset him badly. Which ultimately spoke volumes about their own marriage and where it was heading.

Rosie burned with jealousy every time she saw Marguerite, whether she was with Jack or her father. Her best friend had won the hearts of the only two men that Rosie had ever loved. It was so unfair. If only they had waited a little longer Rosie could at least have claimed her father as her own for a while and run back to the comfort of his unquestioning love. Now she had no one to turn to. She found herself envying Emma. Emma had Jack's love. And his shoulder to cry on. And his care and concern whenever life left her nowhere else to turn. Rosie had nothing. Except her work. And Jack begrudged her even that.

She was in the poolhouse watching the tiles go up one miserable afternoon when Jack appeared. She was glad

that the weather was grey and damp. It made the impact
of the tiles even greater.

'They look good, don't they?' she said, smiling with
pride.

He looked around distractedly. 'Great.' His voice
lacked conviction, as she had known it would.

Then he turned to her and said softly, 'Come into my
study with me. There's something I want to discuss.'

Rosie followed him, feeling nervous. There had been
something ominous in his tone. Was he going to ask her
to leave? If he did, she resolved, then she'd insist that
he loan her the money for a deposit on a small flat. He'd
been the one who insisted that she stay with him and
give it a try. Had it not been for him she would still be
living in her own family home, excitedly preparing for
the wedding. It was his fault that living with her father's
new wife was going to be an impossible ordeal. She would
refuse to feel guilty about asking for a loan.

He took up his seat at his desk, leaving her to take
the chair opposite. It all seemed horribly formal. She
ran her tongue over her lips, waiting.

'Your father's wedding . . .' he began gravely, leaning
back in his chair and surveying her through narrowed
eyes. 'He's written to Emma asking her to attend. She
won't.'

'Oh . . .' said Rosie weakly, too relieved that he wasn't
giving her her marching orders to think of much else for
a moment.

'Is that all you have to say?'

Rosie blinked. 'It's a shame,' she said, trying to gather
her wits together. 'Dad will be very disappointed, I'm
sure.'

Jack closed his eyes briefly, then continued in icy
tones, 'I'd like you to write and tell her that. And ask
her yourself to come.'

'Sure. I'll do it now...' she said, feeling strangely light-headed. Oh, thank goodness she didn't have to go yet. She was a weak, crazy, mindless fool to want to stay with him when it was so pointless. But she did, and that was that. Of course, it couldn't go on much longer, but perhaps when the wedding was over next week she would feel less confused. At least the house would be empty for a couple of weeks during the honeymoon. Rosie could go back there then, perhaps, if he decided he'd had enough by then. It would give her a little breathing-space while she looked for a flat. And in the meantime she could share his bed for just a little longer...

Jack had opened a drawer in the desk and produced some paper. He handed her his own fountain-pen, and then got up and left.

His chair, when she sat in it, was still warm. She rubbed the pen along her upper lip, before unscrewing the cap. It smelt of ink, mixed with a faint citrus tang.

As she bent her head to the blank sheet of paper one finger rubbed anxiously at the bridge of her nose. Emma. Oh, dear. How she wished she had a loving sister to confide in and to trust. A hot tear rolled wistfully down her nose. She wiped it away with the back of her hand.

'Dear Emma,' she wrote. What on earth could she put? She thought of her father, so happy at last to be marrying Marguerite. And the stoic way he had withstood the departure of his first wife and elder daughter. He deserved his heart's desire, if anyone did. Another tear dripped from the end of her nose. 'Please, please, please come,' she added. And then so many tears began to fall that she couldn't write any more. With difficulty she scrawled, 'Your sister, Rosie...' and hastily shoved the piece of paper in an envelope and sealed it.

There was to be a pre-nuptial drink in the Farmer's Arms on the day before the wedding. All the locals were there.

Drinks had been lined up on the bar, awaiting them.
Jack was there, too, at Marguerite's special request. Rosie
didn't know whether to laugh or cry when he said he'd
come. She hadn't been able to persuade him near her
father once.

The happy couple's happiness was so evident that the
whole pub seemed to be full of it. Rosie wandered aimlessly, accepting belated congratulations on her own
marriage from people she'd known all her life. She was
kept busy, smiling brightly and giving the right wrong
impression. It all seemed to go on forever. Jack and her
father seemed to be getting on famously under
Marguerite's tutelage. It should have been a sight to
gladden Rosie's heart, but the knowledge that Marguerite
had succeeded where she had failed clouded her view.
At last she drifted out into the car park. The air was
fresh and clean, damp against her cheeks. She went back
in and found Jack.

'Can we go home, Jack?' she asked bleakly.

He frowned at her. Then, surprisingly, he smiled and
put his arm around her shoulder and took her out to the
car.

'Weren't you enjoying yourself, Rosie?' he asked.

She shrugged. 'It was a good do. But I'd suddenly had
enough.'

He kept his arm around her, until she was safely in
her seat, and then smiled before closing the door and
coming around to his side of the car. Why was he in
such a good mood all of a sudden?

When the car was moving Rosie said, 'Jack, I want
to call it a day. Don't contradict me and insist on having
your own way as usual. We've tried it your way, and it's
getting worse, not better. I shan't move out until after
the wedding, of course. I don't want to cause any upset
at a time like this. But I'll get a flat in Dorchester as
soon as I can manage it.'

He glanced across at her. 'What's brought this about?' he enquired sharply.

Oh, dear. He wasn't even trying to contradict her this time. She shrugged. 'Marguerite and Dad, I think. Did you know that Dad chiselled Marguerite a ring out of marble? She won't wear it, but she doesn't mind that it's so horrible. She says they're only for show, really. Do you remember what you said when you gave me my engagement ring? You said it was an important symbol. I...I was impressed by your saying that. I'd like to think that one day there might be...another ring.' It cost her a lot to say that. She couldn't bear to think of Jack loving someone else, but she did want him to be happy. 'Dad found happiness second time around. It isn't impossible, you know.'

There was a long silence. Jack pulled the car into the open gateway of a field, stopping it on the carpet of mud inside the entrance. On the far side of the field a tractor ploughed a straight furrow, back and forth, patient against the grey sky. When he spoke his voice was deep and resonant, not hard. 'I don't know what to say...' he murmured.

'That's my line,' muttered Rosie, greyly.

He made a soft, appreciative noise in the back of his throat. 'I liked your father very much,' he said at last. 'He and Marguerite will be good for each other.'

'Yes,' she agreed, puzzled by his avoidance of the subject. It wasn't like Jack to shy away from important issues.

He sighed. 'They'll both have to change if they're to make a go of it, though.'

'Ah...' she said, light dawning. 'I see. Yes, they both know that they'll have to adapt. And they love each other so they want to. But Marguerite will still go on being Marguerite and Dad will still be Dad. The changes will be superficial in comparison to what you're asking me to do.'

'I don't think so, Rosie,' he said quietly. 'I had quite an eye-opener meeting your father today. I'd often wondered about him. All these tales of his famous bad temper... And your mother. She's a lovely person. I used to ask myself what kind of a man could have just let her walk out like that without trying to get her back. And then again, Emma had given me an impression of a very different man. Weak and selfish and manipulating. It was a teenager's view of him, formed at a time when she was young and vulnerable.'

'Is that how she saw Dad?' exclaimed Rosie, stunned. Slowly she continued, 'She'd just reached a stage where she was beginning to rebel. I used to stand up for Dad... try to explain... She accused me once of being in his power... But I thought she was just in a foul mood and saying the first thing that came into her head. I never believed she really thought Dad was like that!'

'Everyone needs to make the emotional break from their parents at some time. It can be a hard experience. If Emma had stayed where she was, no doubt she would have realised...'

'Emma certainly made the break in style,' muttered Rosie.

'You were very young too, at the time. Don't you think that you too might be stuck with some ideas which should have served their purpose long ago?'

Rosie looked at him. His eyes were fixed on the tractor. 'You want me to change, Jack. You want me to be less the person I am, more the person you would like me to be. But falling in love with you was more than a teenage aberration. It's not something I can grow out of.'

'That wasn't what I meant,' he said, and there was, for once, a keen note of despair in his words. He started the engine. 'I'll buy you a house, Rosie,' he said. 'With a garden of your own. You're right. There isn't any point any more...'

Rosie's eyes went out to the sky. Grey. Comforting. Big. Scratched and scarred by the bare branches of trees around its edges. Thick and blanketing in the middle. Beyond it, somewhere, shone a sun.

When they got back to the house Jack took her to their room and made love with her. In daylight, with his eyes open. When they lay spent upon the bed, Rosie didn't reach for her robe. She didn't have to be ashamed of her need any more. They were parting. This was a goodbye gift. She could accept it with grace.

The next day Jack should have been up at the crack of dawn, on his way to Milan and a meeting so important that it couldn't be postponed. When Rosie awoke at eight he was still beside her in the bed.

'I'm coming with you to the wedding,' he said. And somehow his change of heart made everything seem even more final.

The civil ceremony was soon over, and everyone milled around outside while the photographer tried to impose some sort of order on a group of mature and spirited guests.

Danny's arm came around Rosie's shoulder. 'I'm glad Jack made it, after all. It shows how much he thinks of you. That meeting of his was very important...'

'Yes,' agreed Rosie, weakly.

'Shame about Emma, though,' he muttered. 'Still, discovering that Colin Hellec was her natural father like that when she was only seventeen...' He sucked on his teeth. 'Naturally she looks on him as her father in every sense of the word these days. It's just foolish old me that still thinks of her as my daughter. I told your mother right from the start that it would make no difference to me... A baby was a baby, when all was said and done. But it didn't seem that way to poor Em when she found

out. She wanted to be with her natural parents, and who
can blame the girl . . . ?'

At which point the dismayed photographer, discovering the groom mumbling away to some beautiful young
woman while his new wife posed flirtatiously with all
and sundry, grabbed hold of Danny's arm and forced
him to kiss the bride for the birdie—leaving a stunned
Rosie blinking hard into the watery rays of the sun.

Finally everyone got into their cars to head for the
parish church where the wedding was to be blessed. Jack
pulled away in front of the others and drove brusquely,
his features set. Did he really love Marguerite? Had it
been so hard watching her get married, after all? Rosie
felt too devastated to care much any more.

They were the first to arrive at the church. The vicar
was waiting at the altar. There were a few villagers
already in the church, sitting at the back. And a single
figure sitting near the front like a proper guest, a figure
with light brown hair, cut short around a pale, freckled
face. It was Emma. Emma looking grown-up and
worried and tired. Rosie felt a prickle of dismay run
through her. She wasn't ready to face Emma right now.
What had Dad said? She was sure she hadn't misheard,
but there hadn't been a chance to question him and the
bare information seemed too scant. It needed fleshing
out before it could become real, somehow. Rosie glanced
up at Jack. His face was unreadable. Anxiously she
started to make her way to the far side of the church.
She could ask her father more at the reception, and then
talk to Emma when it all made sense.

But Jack had other ideas. His fingers closed over her
arm and he began to lead her firmly towards the front
where her sister was sitting. He pushed her into the pew
beside Emma, and then followed himself.

Rosie and Emma looked uncertainly at each other.

'Rosie?' whispered Emma, her grey eyes pleading.

'Oh...' The sound caught in her throat, muffled by emotion.

Emma looked nervously away. Rosie, too, found her eyes travelling to the front of the church. Emma was only her half-sister. And not Jack's stepsister, but *his* half-sister, too. She frowned, trying to work out how it all must have come about. And then the organ crashed into life and Marguerite made her grand entrance, smiling an orchid-blush smile, while Danny grinned from an unfamiliarly clean-shaven face. Rosie smoothed her hair back from her face. They were the important ones right now. This was their moment. This was her own father, bright-eyed, loving, standing up there with his bride. For the present she would give him all her attention. The rest of it could wait.

Now and again, though, she glanced at Jack. How she wished he could look at her as her father was looking at Marguerite. But he just stared impassively straight ahead, keeping up the façade for one last day. At last the happy couple were walking back up the aisle and out into the pale sunlight.

Rosie turned to Emma. 'Why didn't you answer my letter and tell me you were coming?' she asked a little stiffly, not really knowing what she should say.

'There wasn't time,' said Emma nervously.

Rosie looked at her with a rush of long-forgotten affection. She gave Emma a rueful smile. 'You're *not* my sister,' she found herself saying wonderingly, eager now to mend every last stick of the broken fence. 'It was only back there, just now, talking to Dad—er—Danny, I mean, because, of course——'

But before she could knock the first paling home Jack's fingers bit fiercely into her arm. She turned, bewildered, to face him. His eyes were hard mirrors. He turned an unyielding face on her and said harshly, 'I can't stand any more of this. You're coming with me.'

Rosie swung her head around to look at Emma, and then at her father and Marguerite, being photographed in the porch.

'No... Please... Jack... Don't upset things now...'

This time there wasn't even a pretence of protective courtesy. He pulled her roughly behind him, and out through the side-door. They were in the car and roaring back to Littlebourne before anyone except Emma knew that they had gone.

Rosie swallowed hard. 'Couldn't you have left me there to enjoy my own father's wedding?'

'No.'

'Jack, when did your father first meet my mother?'

The car drew to a halt at a crossroads. The face that Jack turned on her was white with anger. His eyes blazed cold and hard. 'What sort of damn fool question is that?' he jeered. 'Now shut up. I don't think I can bear to listen to the sound of your voice.'

CHAPTER ELEVEN

'BUT Jack...!'

'Shut up!' There was such a welter of fury in his voice that she did as he bid her, fearful for her own safety if she were to annoy him further while he was behind the wheel of the car.

At last the car swung aggressively in at the gates of Littlebourne and jolted to a vicious halt in front of the steps. The Virginia creeper had shed its red leaves almost overnight. They gusted wildly across their path as Jack pulled her towards the house.

'Jack. Please. What's going on? You're hurting my arm... Please...'

'I feel like hurting a damned sight more than your arm, you little bitch.'

'I don't understand...'

'Nor do I. I don't understand how I can go on feeling this way about you... even after all this time. Even knowing that nothing will change you. God damn you, Rosie! How could I have allowed you to get to me like this?'

'Jack!' She was frightened now. He was actually quaking with anger. She could feel it in the callous bite of his hand against her flesh. 'Please let go of me...' she said shakily.

He cast her a look of derision, but freed her arm.

She stood still, overcome with a mixture of fear and relief. Should she run away now, while she had the chance?

He turned back to survey her. 'Come with me. I'm not going to hurt you.'

'You already have.'

He shrugged carelessly. 'I shan't touch you again, Rosie. You don't need to worry about that.'

She hesitated, bewildered and shocked, then reluctantly followed him into the house. He started up the stairs.

'Come on,' he urged.

'I... No, if you don't mind you can say whatever it is you want to say down here. I'd feel safer.'

His eyebrows puckered with cold exasperation. 'I've already told you that I shan't touch you. I'm only going upstairs because that's where you keep your belongings. I thought I'd help you pack. But if you'd rather I'll pack them for you. It will be my pleasure.'

'I...' She swallowed hard, feeling almost sick with self-disgust. How on earth could she have been so stupid as to get embroiled with him again? She followed him upstairs, though. She wanted the dignity of packing her own bags and leaving. Being dumped on the doorstep with all her worldly possessions would be a little hard to stomach.

'What's brought all this on, Jack?' she asked stiffly, as they went into their bedroom.

Jack said nothing at first. He just opened the door to the dressing-room and began to bring armfuls of her clothes through and dump them on the bed.

'Tell me!' Rosie insisted shrilly.

But he replied only with a look of frozen disdain.

'Is it Marguerite? Couldn't you bear to see her getting married? Is that it?'

'What the hell has Marguerite got to do with any of this? She may be a tough nut, but your father very obviously loves her. They'll be happy. It's just an everyday story of love and marriage. I envy her that. But why should it bother me?'

'Then why?' Rosie despised herself for the relief she felt at his words. She *wouldn't* love him any more. She *wouldn't* let herself care. 'Why did you drag me away? Tell me!'

Jack dropped the clothes insolently on the bed, then turned to face her. He looked at her with such pent-up anger that she felt frightened again. 'I couldn't stand there and listen for another moment,' he said disdainfully. 'I'd had enough.'

'So what was it you couldn't bear hearing, Jack?' she said as evenly as she could manage, not wanting to hear his reply.

'You,' he accused, his voice low. 'You, of course. You have the capacity to be one of the most loving and generous of people on the face of this earth... I see you with other people—your father, Marguerite, Aubrey... It chokes me to see you with them. I can't bear it. Because I'm also forced to look at this other side—this parody... this... this twisted little wretch, eaten up with bitterness and enjoying it! The woman who stood by my side in the church back there and said, "You're not my sister"——!' He broke off, his face hard. 'But not any longer, Rosie. I'm not going to stand by and watch it any more.'

He cast her a look of savage condemnation. Then he turned and stormed into the dressing-room, returning with a suitcase, which he flung carelessly on the floor. 'Start packing,' he bit out. 'I don't care where you spend the night, as long as it's not under the same roof as me.'

'But all I meant...' she protested, her face stiff and white. Then she stopped herself. How in heaven could he believe she was like that? Of course she had been hurt in the past—and yes, she *had* felt bitter. But she had never looked for revenge—never relished her wounds.

Never looked for sympathy, nor sought to justify herself in other people's eyes. His accusation was way off the mark.

'Ah, Rosie...' His face was flushed now and his eyes burned fierce blue against the dark hue of his skin. 'Why did you do it? Why do you keep on doing it? Why do you let it all fester inside you? It burns me up...' His fists clenched hard. 'But that's nothing to what I see it doing to you. It's poisoning you. You'll end up hating me before long, Rosie. I've no doubt you'll end up blaming me for some imagined hurt all the days of your life. But I'm not sticking around to watch the show.'

Rosie looked at him, her eyes round and blank with shock. 'No...' she protested through dry lips. 'Jack, I was starting to make things up...to mend fences. I won't deny that I——'

'I was there!' he jeered, incredulously. 'I saw it. I heard you!'

How could she explain? And why did she want to when he was so...so...? He hated her. Why should she want him to understand? Yet still her mouth kept repeating, 'Jack? Please...please, Jack.'

But he brushed furiously past her, flinching as his arm knocked against hers. He turned to look coldly into her eyes. 'You accused me once of having taught my eyes to lie for me. I thought such a thing was impossible. But I was wrong. *You've* done it. And not just your eyes but your face, Rosie...all that injured innocence in the set of your mouth... But in there...in your heart where it really matters, there's nothing but a...a solid fist of stone. I've refused to let myself believe it for too long. But I believe it now, Rosie. You'll never take me in again. It's over. I just want you out of this house. Out of my life. Preferably within the next five minutes.'

'In the church...' she said falteringly. 'Jack, listen. In the church when I saw Emma——'

But he cut into her attempts to explain. 'Oh, yes. Sorry,' he said fiercely. 'I remember now. You threw your arms around your long-lost sister and begged her to forgive and forget. I've got it all wrong, haven't I?'

'No. I mean, yes. I mean, I know I didn't do that—but I probably would have done if you'd left me alone for just a few more minutes.'

The scorn which contorted his features was absolute. The contours of his mouth erased themselves, leaving a hard white line in their place. His brow seemed cleft in two by the severity of the frown line which manifested itself there. And his eyes...oh, his eyes. They were as cold as the fathomless wastes of the moon.

'So now you've taken to lying as well. At least until now I've credited you with honesty.'

'I *am* being honest.'

He closed his eyes and screwed up his face. '*Don't*,' he roared. 'I thought you'd hurt me all you could when you left the first time round. When you said you didn't love me, that you only wanted to use me...for sex. I convinced myself that you were too young. Too young to tie yourself down to being a wife. Too young to understand how much I needed you—or to know what real love was. But I thought you'd grow up, Rosie. That you'd taste life at university—meet other men. And then you'd come back to me... You'd learn that the way we were together was something very special.

'But when you didn't come...I thought... Oh, hell, who cares what I thought? Until that friend of Emma's said that her brother called you "the perpetual virgin"! That was when I bought this house. I hoped... I thought that if life hadn't opened your eyes yet, then I would have to come and do it myself. I was so full of hope. I was so sure that you just needed love and time and all your wounds would heal. But I was wrong. So don't lie to me, Rosie. At least leave me that. Just go now before you do anything more to hurt me.'

'Stop it!' Her fists came up to her forehead and clamped themselves to her temples. 'Stop it! Stop it!' she wailed, her voice shredded with pain. 'Please, Jack, listen!'

'No.' And he went once more to the dressing-room.

Rosie was shaking so badly she couldn't stand. She took a few elderly steps to the edge of the bed and slumped into a sitting position.

The next lot of clothes hit her back, sleeves escaping from the bundle to slap unkindly at her. She was scarcely aware of them. She wouldn't try any more to make him listen. There was no point. He loathed her, anyway, no matter what she said. It would do no good, and perhaps it would be easier, after she'd gone, if she knew that there was no hope, no chance at all. She sat frozen, trying to breathe normally, fighting against the storm of grief which threatened to swallow her.

'Poor wretch,' muttered Jack without compassion. 'Sitting there, so pathetic and lost. But you don't fool me, Rosie. Not any more.'

'When . . . ?' Rosie's lips seemed to be forming the words automatically, without any guidance from within. 'When did your father first meet my mother?'

Jack let out a shuddering sigh. 'What does that have to do with anything?'

'Please . . . I beg you, Jack . . . Just answer me . . .'

He shrugged. 'I don't know. A long time ago. I was eight or nine, I think.'

'And Emma is your father's child?'

'Stop it!' He exclaimed angrily. 'All this is just delaying tactics, isn't it? You know all that already. Now get packing . . .' And he flicked a bunch of keys out of his pocket and threw open the case.

It was his case. The one he always used. And it had already been packed in preparation for the Milan trip. He scooped out his clothes and began throwing them on the floor. There was a thud. Among the tangle of shirts and socks appeared a glimpse of worn red leather. It was her mother's jewel-case.

'Oh...' she gasped, falling on her knees and reaching for it. The little silver key was still in the lock.

He poked at it with his toe. 'Yours, I believe,' he said disdainfully. 'It's all yours, Rosie. I've carried it with me for four years, waiting for you to come to me and ask for it back. For these past weeks I've been waiting for you to ask me to put your rings back on your finger. It seems I have no further need of it.' And suddenly across his face flashed a look of such bleak despair that Rosie almost cried out.

Mindlessly she turned the key and opened it. There, on top, was a familiar little white box. It was already open. Her rings gleamed softly in the winter's light. She slammed the box shut, then looked wildly up at Jack.

'Listen to me...Jack, please, please listen to me...' Rosie didn't actually know what she wanted to say to him. But suddenly she felt with a dreadful urgency that she was fighting for her life. Either she found the words now and spoke them, or she would lose the man she loved forever and ever. Just moments ago she had believed that it was better that they parted. That although it would break her heart it would set Jack free to find someone else. Now she knew that the only freedom either of them would find if she went was the freedom to grieve all the days of their lives.

'I love you, Jack...I love you so much,' she said.

Dammit. Not the right words. His expression of frozen disdain deepened. 'So you keep saying,' he jeered. 'It doesn't seem to mean an awful lot. It evaporated the moment you saw me with Emma.'

'Because I thought you were lovers! You know that! And it came back the moment I discovered that I'd been wrong.'

He shook his head coldly. 'It's exactly as I said. It's a poor love, Rosie, that's so easily scared away. For goodness' sake, I'd just come from our marriage bed. How could you have thought that just because I had my arm round Emma that we were lovers? How could you have had so little faith?'

Still not the right words. Oh, where were they? Rosie got to her feet and went to stand close to him, looking challengingly into his eyes. 'Because,' she said staunchly, taking a deep breath, 'I believed something much worse of you than that. It was something she said that day. And, of course, ever since I found out you were brother and sister it's seemed too absurd to mention. I . . . I was appalled at myself for having believed it. But you must believe me, Jack, when I tell you that it made sense at the time. I honestly thought it was true, you see. I really did.'

She paused, taking another steadying breath. 'I . . . I believed that you had married me because Emma was infertile. That you wanted me to bear the child she couldn't have.' She swallowed hard.

But her painful confession only brought another ironic smile to his lips. 'Oh, my God,' he groaned. 'This gets increasingly ridiculous. Can't you think up better lies than that, Rosie?'

'It's not a lie!'

He sighed. 'Well, if Emma's infertile then it's the first I've heard of it. She's always on about the huge family she plans to have when the time comes. And I certainly don't remember her begging me to persuade you to act as a surrogate mother for her! All she wanted to know was when I was going to sort things out between the two of you so that she could offer you her heartfelt congratulations.'

Rosie's mind began to grind faster. She was almost on the edge of panic. She was failing. His heart was closed. He wouldn't listen, wouldn't understand.

'Jack,' she pleaded desperately, 'she'd had appendicitis. I'd read somewhere—anyway, I thought maybe it had left her unable to have children. You see... Oh, Jack, please think. Please try to remember that day. What she said. Please think back.' Frightened by the harsh set of his features, she clutched at his shirt-front, her fingers knotted, and tried to shake him. But he stood granite-still. 'She said... Jack, she said... Oh, please try to remember... She said, "Is she pregnant yet?" and you said, "Patience, patience..." And then she said, "I know I'm being absurd, but I can't wait to be an... well, I shall be a good deal more than an *aunt* when the time comes, won't I? It will be *your* child, Jack, not just Rosie's. Oh, anyone can have a common-or-garden niece or nephew, can't they? But this baby will be practically the same as one of my own. Do you blame me for being excited at the prospect? Oh, I can't wait for the three of us to be together..."' Her voice dropped to a pleading whisper. 'Oh, think, Jack, please think. You must remember... Oh, please...'

'How,' he said faintly at last, his face appalled, 'how the hell did you remember all that? I'd quite forgotten.'

Rosie stumbled towards the bed and sat on the edge, shaking almost uncontrollably. 'I... It was very important to me. At the time. And, to be honest, I didn't know I was word-perfect until it all came pouring out just then. You see, they were the words which shattered my life. They were the words which made me say all those spiteful things and made me throw your rings at you and made me tell you again and again that I hated you when you walked back into my life. Do you see now

why I was so very bitter, and why discovering the truth
made such a big difference to me?'

He came weakly to sit beside her on the edge of the
bed, frowning. 'Why didn't you tell me?' he said.

She let out a shuddering sigh. 'I might have. If you'd
loved me too. If we could have lain in bed and laughed
away my foolishness. But when I told you that I loved
you again you were so cold and distant. And I knew you
didn't love me. And I couldn't somehow make myself
form the words which might have sounded my death-
knell. I couldn't see how I could tell you how badly I'd
misjudged you. I was afraid you'd be disgusted and send
me away.'

'I wouldn't have sent you away.'

'Wouldn't you? You're sending me away now, Jack.'

He blew out a heavy sigh, slowly shaking his head.
'Yes,' he agreed slowly. 'I am. I've finally given up on
you...us... But I hadn't done then.'

'Would it have made a difference if I'd told you all
that stuff about the baby sooner?' she asked, managing
to keep her voice firm. She had been wrong about the
jewel-case. Horribly wrong. Still, she had to know. Later,
she would need to know.

He shook his head. 'No. Not really. Or at least I don't
think so. It makes it all a little more... understandable.
I mean, I understand now why you were so cruel when
you went. Why you said those things. But I don't believe
you've really changed, Rosie. I wish I could. I've been
kidding myself all this time that things would come right,
but it hasn't worked. Do you remember that very first
day, when you were so... so brittle about your mother?
All that stuff about her being ecstatically happy...? I
knew then that this bitterness ran very deep, Rosie. But
then you were so vulnerable, so young. It was hardly
surprising. Emma knew you were angry with her, especially as you'd been left alone with your father.

Remember, I thought your father was a pretty difficult man at that time.' He shrugged. 'Now I know that he's not, it makes it all seem that much more inevitable. His love hasn't been able to heal you, either. Once I'd met him I knew I was fighting a lost cause.'

'Oh, Jack. I don't know what to say. That first day I said all that stuff about my mother because I was so desperate to impress you. That was all.'

He shook his head. 'But you can't forgive Emma, Rosie.' He shrugged. 'She's grown up now. She doesn't need me to protect her any more. So in a way it's immaterial to me how you feel about her. But the trouble is, I'm tainted in your eyes by the hatred you bear her, aren't I? I've begged you to put all that bitterness behind you. To free yourself to learn what *real* love was all about. The way that I've loved you all these years, Rosie.' He laid his hand tenderly over hers. 'But you can't change. And unless you do you'll never love me the way I need you to love me...I can't live with second-best. I've tried and it's no good.'

'Jack...' whispered Rosie faintly, not bothering to contradict him. 'Today I discovered for the very first time that Emma is your father's natural child. Before that I thought she was his stepdaughter. Now I understand at last why she felt she had to beg Mum to give her love a chance. And I've forgiven her everything—not that there really was anything to forgive, of course.' She stopped and took in a weary breath. 'I don't expect you to believe that, or to understand exactly what it means, but at least I've said it. For the record. You can pass the message on to Emma.' Suddenly her hands dropped and she looked up at Jack. She had given up struggling to find the right words. Any minute now she would start folding up all those clothes and laying them in the case.

Jack stared and stared. And then the tension locking his muscles seemed to disperse. His hand came up to rub at his face.

'I think I'm beginning to see.' He paused. 'You mean that you thought Emma was responsible for breaking up your family? With no good reason?'

'Yes.'

'Oh, Rosie.' He let out a long sigh. 'I couldn't believe that you really loved me as you claimed to. Not when you couldn't set the past aside for my sake. "Won't you change?" That's what I said, time and again.'

'I...' Rosie's eyes were blank, empty. When she turned them on him she couldn't make them focus. 'Change? Is that what you meant by my changing?'

'Yes. That was all I wanted—for you to let go of all that hurt. Of course, I thought that you knew why Emma had wanted to go, and you were being obtuse. But... Well, dammit, Rosie. You must have known what I wanted. What else could I possibly have meant?'

Rosie's brows curved into wide, astonished arcs. 'Good grief. That's not what I thought you meant at all. I didn't need to change inside, you see. I loved you, and I couldn't help that. And I certainly didn't *want* to feel the way that I did about Emma. But I didn't seem to have much choice. I couldn't imagine that you'd expect me to be able to change that!'

'Rosie?' For the first time there was an anxious note of uncertainty in his voice.

'Actually,' she found herself saying, 'what I thought you wanted me to do was to become a more suitable sort of... well, consort for a man like you. You see, when you admired that yellow dress of mine you said you thought I'd become sharper and cooler. I thought you liked that. And you wished that I'd gone to university, which probably would have made me even sharper and even cooler in your eyes. You wanted me to buy lots of clothes and give up work and talk about current affairs. I thought you were hoping I'd change into a sort of a sophisticated mistress-cum-hostess type of woman. You know, the sort who has a manicurist call to the house and arranges dinner parties all the time. I thought you wanted me to stop being me.

'After all, *you'd* changed. I mean, you used to have that cream sports car and you used to laugh and bring me droopy bunches of wild flowers and everything. Only now you're much more...oh, you know. Sombre. A tough businessman driving a gloomy hearse of a car, eating all the right foods in the right restaurants, and being good at charming people. Do you remember that Thai restaurant, Jack, where we didn't know how to eat that particular dish, and the waiter was so polite and didn't say anything and then we saw the couple at the next table eating it with their fingers and we laughed because we'd asked for chopsticks and got in such a mess? That's the sort of people we used to be then— relaxed and open together. Now I feel as if I don't know you. As if we don't match any more, except between the sheets and even then...' She sighed, frowning.

'Anyway, to get back to the point, I thought that as you didn't love me any more, but you were determined to hang on to me as a wife, then you must want me to alter myself to fit the part... Actually, it made a lot of sense.' She looked worriedly across at Jack. His face was impassive, his grave blue eyes fixed on her.

'Why are you letting me rabbit on, Jack? Usually you can't bear it when I start to talk like this.'

He looked very intently into her eyes. His hands came up to her shoulders, holding her firmly but gently. Then he stood up, drawing her to her feet beside him. He swallowed hard. 'Because I love it when you talk like that. Go on talking, Rosie. Just go on talking as you were just then.'

'I don't know what to say,' she whispered, uncertainly.

'Shall we save the talking for later?' he murmured. He swallowed so hard that his Adam's apple moved visibly in his throat. She put up a hand and laid it tenderly on the spot.

'When you started to get enthusiastic about your work,' he continued, 'you forgot to be cold and distant, and you would start chattering on, just as you did a few moments ago. It was you speaking then, Rosie. The real you. The you that I craved with every breath that I took. The you that I thought I couldn't have. I couldn't bear it. I'm not a masochist.'

'I—er—oh, dear...' Rosie's chin was beginning to pucker ominously, and her eyes were stinging. She could feel the hum of his words in his throat through her fingertips. She could sense the warm movement of air they made soft against her hair. She could hear them in her ears, believe them in her heart. She lifted her hand to do what she had been longing to do since first she set eyes on him all those weeks before—she stroked his hair. She let her fingers trace the grey streaks. Then she rested her cheek against his chest and closed her eyes, letting the sweet tears of relief seep between her lashes.

He gathered her to him with such an abundance of tenderness that the tears began to fall even faster. Then he freed one hand and used it to toss the bedspread with its burden of clothes on to the floor. He led her to the bed and sat her down. And then he began to kiss her.

He kissed her cheeks, very gently, very lightly. And he licked away the salt tears with the tip of his tongue.

She laughed shakily. 'You stick out your tongue like that when you eat toast. I couldn't bear to watch it...' she muttered.

'Do I?' he murmured against her skin, pushing her backwards on to the bed.

'Yes. You don't butter your toast and bite it, you see——'

But his lips were dancing against hers now, silencing her. She closed her eyes again and let her mind drift. This breath against her mouth was his breath. This chin, rough against her cheek, was his chin. This heart she felt beating through their clothes was his heart. His heart, given to her. She opened her eyes a crack, and let the colour of his skin swim in front of her eyes. The kiss deepened, his tongue probing gently over her lips and into her mouth. This kiss was their kiss. How could she have forgotten?

They undressed each other slowly, sitting cross-legged opposite each other on the bed, smiling. He unpinned her hair. She fumbled with the knot of his tie, until he dislodged her clumsy fingers and tore it impatiently open. And all the while they looked and smiled.

When they were naked she whispered, 'Turn around, Jack. Let me look at your back.'

Laughingly, he did as he was bid, stretching out on his side on the bed. She knelt beside him, just looking. The moles and freckles on the smooth expanse of olive skin were just exactly where they had always been. She bent her head and kissed each blemish with infinite tenderness. The hairs sprinkled across his shoulders and in the small of his back tickled her cheek, sending a shudder of desire racing through her. She lay down beside him, on her side too, leaning her body against his long back, feeling the hard curve of his buttocks press against her thighs. She slipped her hands around his waist and let her tongue trail wantonly against the nape of his neck.

He groaned. 'Stop it,' he implored. 'It's too delicious. I'd forgotten. I want this to last forever, but if you keep doing that I'll lose control.

She rolled over on to her back and smiled. Propping himself on one elbow, he turned towards her and looked

into her eyes. And then slowly he unfolded himself and
stood up and crossed the room. He stooped to open the
jewel-case, and came back to her with the little white
box in his hand. 'Symbolic,' he murmured as he slipped
the sapphire and diamond ring on to her finger, 'of all
the beautiful days and nights promised between us.' And
then he took out the gold band and added, ' "With my
body I thee worship. . ." ' And then he began to kiss her
again. To worship her, as she did him.

Worshipfully, eyes wide open, he moved his mouth
down over her throat and to her breasts. Lightly he kissed
her throbbing nipples, letting his lips brush over them,
before teasing them into greater prominence with the tip
of his tongue. Then he drew first one nipple and then
the other deep into his mouth, sucking hard upon their
swollen peaks, until she trembled and shook with desire.

'Oh. . .like that. . .just like that. . .I remember now. . .'
she urged, her voice soft and sweet with love.

'And this,' he murmured thickly, laying his cheek upon
her breast and taking her hand. Quivering with antici-
pation, she allowed him to touch her fingertips to the
petal-soft tip of his manhood. 'Remember this,
Rosie. . . ?' he groaned.

Try as they might, they couldn't make their lovemaking last forever. Each remembered gesture, each
glimpse of the other, naked and proud in daylight,
brought a fresh surge of clamouring need to their bodies.
A hot urgency began to suck at Rosie, pulling her towards him, fastening her fingers to his flesh, her lips to
his mouth.

Shaking, he pulled back, stroking at her hair with his
long fingers. The blue eyes which met hers were misted
with desire. 'Now,' he whispered. 'It has to be now. . .
I can't wait. . .'

She closed her eyes, yearning for their bodies to
become one. He entered her slowly, sending the blood

thundering through her veins, drawing the breath from her lungs, loosing a wild music in her ears. And then he thrust hard, tipping her raging senses into a sea of perfect calm. She felt herself close around him, while her mind streamed into that timeless space. The colour she saw behind her closed lids was, this time, whiter than light, made brilliant by starpoints of ecstasy.

Afterwards they stayed locked in each other's arms, their fingers tracing the contours of ears and mouths, their lips brushing restlessly against each other's skin, until they found they were making love all over again.

Getting back into her clothes was desperately difficult, with Jack trying to kiss her breasts as she fumbled with her buttons. 'Later,' she grinned, 'I shall pay you back for all this. But if we miss any more of Dad's wedding I shall never forgive you.'

And then he swung her into the air and kissed her hard on the lips, and said, 'Never forgive me? Oh, don't tell lies, Rosie Hellec. It's not in your nature to bear a grudge!'

And then she smiled, and he smiled, and they kept on smiling all the way back to the reception.

'Come with me,' demanded Marguerite, taking Rosie by the hand. 'I want you to show that to your father.'

'All right, Mother,' said Rosie meekly.

Marguerite lifted her hand threateningly, then hastily tucked her open palm behind her back. 'There's a photographer on the prowl,' she explained. 'It wouldn't do to have a wedding photo of the bride smacking her stepdaughter's bottom, now would it? But I warn you, if you ever call me Mother again...'

Danny came up at that moment and hugged his new wife. 'Where on earth did you and Jack get to, Rosie? You've missed all the good bits.'

Marguerite shook her head. 'Judging by the sheepish grins on their faces when they finally arrived, I'd say they've been doing what we plan to be doing a few hours from now.'

Danny rubbed his clean-shaven chin roguishly. 'Can't blame them for that, Marguerite. They're an old married couple by all accounts.' And he winked at Rosie.

'Anyway,' continued Marguerite emphatically, 'what they were or were not up to is hardly the point. Rosie's got something to show you.' And she thrust Rosie's left hand under her father's nose.

'That, Danny, my dear,' she said cynically, 'is what I call an engagement ring. Take note.'

'Not wearing yours, Marguerite, I see...' said Rosie drily.

Marguerite rummaged in her white clutch-purse and extracted a squashed garden glove. She unfolded it to reveal the marble ring squeezed on to the third finger. 'I felt it ought to be shown off in its appropriate habitat,' she said caustically.

It was Danny's turn to look sheepish.

'Now if you've finished admiring my rings, you two,' murmured Rosie, 'you'll have to excuse me. I must go and find my husband.'

'Quite right,' muttered Marguerite. 'Don't let a man like that out of your sight for longer than you have to. Four years was quite long enough...'

Rosie found herself chuckling as she wandered off to seek out Jack. She found him sitting in a quiet corner, sipping champagne with Emma. He got up and tucked his arm possessively around Rosie's waist, drawing her into the circle of warmth which seemed to emanate from him.

'I've been explaining to Em why we won't be inviting her for Christmas this year,' smiled Jack.

Emma grinned warmly. 'It's OK. I can quite understand why you'd choose to spend your first Christmas
together on an island in the Indian Ocean instead of with
me. As it happens I can't think of anything worse than
spending Christmas day with a pair of besotted
lovebirds.'

Rosie and Jack looked besottedly into each other's
eyes while Emma grimaced.

'Don't think, though,' she sighed—and was there just
a tinge of envy in that sigh?—'that you can stay on your
island forever. Dad and Marguerite have invited me over
for New Year. I fully expect you to be around so that
we can see the year in as a family.'

Rosie smiled tenderly at her sister. 'Hmm. You've just
stolen my line. Except that I was going to suggest that
we come to Italy for New Year, and celebrate as a family
there.'

Emma laughed. 'You don't want to start a family row
over it, do you?'

'Tell me!' he demanded cold-bloodedly. 'Tell me this instant or I'll tickle you to within an inch of your life.'

She nuzzled against his naked chest, relishing the
coarseness of the hairs against her cheek. 'I can't,' she
protested. 'You'll think I'm mad. It all sounds so stupid
now.'

He flexed his fingers, then wiggled them over her
midriff. 'Rosie, we've done enough damage by refusing
to talk. Now I'll carry out my threat. I promise,
unless——'

'OK, OK, I give in. I didn't want you to meet him
because . . .' she paused to let out a great gust of laughter
'. . . because,' she gasped, 'I thought you were plotting
with Emma to turn Dad against me. And I needed to
protect him from your evil ways.'

The sound which exploded from his throat would have done credit to Marguerite. He collapsed against the pillows, laughing helplessly. 'Go on,' he taunted at last, 'Tell me more about this plot...'

'Beast!' she hissed, taking advantage of his mirth to tickle his ribs. 'Why shouldn't I have thought that? You were horrible to me. You said such dreadful things.'

'Rubbish...' he muttered, refusing to respond to the tickling.

Rosie sat up and hugged her knees. 'You used to be ticklish,' she complained happily, her eyes narrowing. 'And if you were once, you will be again. I'll just have to train you.'

'Ah...one of those changes you have planned for me.' He was silent for a moment, then reached out his hand and picked up her pack of pills from the table beside the bed. 'There are a few changes I'd like to plan for you, too,' he said contemplatively. 'But I guess it's a bit soon to mention them...'

Rosie took the pills from him. 'You mean...?' She felt her face turn pink.

He smiled up at her, his blue eyes sparkling. 'Well, I would like to change your waist measurement. By at least a foot. But you're a career woman these days. I guess it will have to be you who decides to make that change, not me.'

Rosie frowned. 'Is that why you sent the doctor round that day?' she asked. 'Because of my career?'

He shook his head. 'Not because of your career. But you went on the Pill without saying anything to me, before we even married. I assumed the last thing you wanted was a baby.'

Rosie's shoulders began to quake with laughter. 'I went on the Pill then because of something my father said. Not because I didn't want to get pregnant. You know,

Jack, for such a well-intentioned man, he hasn't half created a lot of problems for us.'

Jack's eyes widened expectantly. 'You mean you wouldn't mind? I mean, correct me if I'm wrong but...'

'But I think my father needs to be paid back for all the damage he's done,' responded Rosie firmly. 'You see, Jack, I *do* have a vindictive streak, after all! Let's see if we can't turn him into a grandfather, and then make him babysit for us at least twice a week.'

Jack beamed, propping himself up on one elbow. 'Good thinking,' he agreed, and then he sat up and stretched. 'But the plan will only work if we create a human dynamo of a child. Perhaps if we put a lot of energy into making her ... it's got to be a girl, you know. They're far more trouble to raise than boys...' And he grabbed Rosie energetically and wrestled her down on to the sheet.

As she closed her eyes against the onslaught of his mouth a decidedly energetic streak of desire leaped inside her. Blue eyes, she willed. Like him. And impeccable taste in men, she added mentally. Like me.

ESCAPE INTO ANOTHER WORLD...

...With Temptation Dreamscape Romances

Two worlds collide in 3 very special Temptation titles, guaranteed to sweep you to the very edge of reality.

The timeless mysteries of reincarnation, telepathy and earthbound spirits clash with the modern lives and passions of ordinary men and women.

Available November 1993   Price £5.55

MILLS & BOON

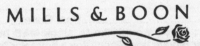

Next Month's Romances

Each month you can choose from a wide variety of romance with Mills & Boon. Below are the new titles to look out for next month, why not ask either Mills & Boon Reader Service or your Newsagent to reserve you a copy of the titles you want to buy – just tick the titles you would like and either post to Reader Service or take it to any Newsagent and ask them to order your books.

Please save me the following titles:		Please tick	✓
TO TAME A WILD HEART	Emma Darcy		
ISLAND ENCHANTMENT	Robyn Donald		
A VALENTINE FOR DAISY	Betty Neels		
PRACTISE TO DECEIVE	Sally Wentworth		
FLAME ON THE HORIZON	Daphne Clair		
ROMAN SPRING	Sandra Marton		
LOVE OR NOTHING	Natalie Fox		
CLOSE CAPTIVITY	Elizabeth Power		
TOTAL POSSESSION	Kathryn Ross		
LOST LADY	Lee Wilkinson		
GIFT-WRAPPED	Victoria Gordon		
NOT SUCH A STRANGER	Liza Hadley		
COLOURS OF LOVE	Rosalie Henaghan		
CHECKMATE	Peggy Nicholson		
TOMORROW'S MAN	Sue Peters		
OF RASCALS AND RAINBOWS	Marcella Thompson		

If you would like to order these books in addition to your regular subscription from Mills & Boon Reader Service please send £1.80 per title to: Mills & Boon Reader Service, Freepost, P.O. Box 236, Croydon, Surrey, CR9 9EL, quote your Subscriber No:.................................... (If applicable) and complete the name and address details below. Alternatively, these books are available from many local Newsagents including W.H.Smith, J.Menzies, Martins and other paperback stockists from 5 November 1993.

Name:...

Address:..

....Post Code:.........................

To Retailer: If you would like to stock M&B books please contact your regular book/magazine wholesaler for details.

You may be mailed with offers from other reputable companies as a result of this application. If you would rather not take advantage of these opportunities please tick box

☐